APACI
GOLD

by Craig Brackenridge

APACHE GOLD
by
Craig Brackenridge

An Old Dogs Publishing Paperback.
First published in Great Britain in 2020 by Old Dog Publishing
5 Hogshill Lane, Cobham KT11 2AG
1st Edition 2020
Copyright © 2020 Craig Brackenridge

Printed with love by DG3 London

A big yee-haw to Bob (The Black Mountain Puma), Butch (The Tall Rider), Dave (The Blackness Wrangler) and Keith (The Airdrie Rustler).

Thanks for inspiration to The Piccadilly Cowboys, Lee Van Cleef, Franco Nero, Thomas Milian, Anthony Steffan and the three Sergio's (Leone, Corbucci and Sollima).

Respect once again to the three amigos that pushed me onto the writing trail: Garry Bushell, Paul Hallam and Alan Wilson.

Many thanks for another astonishing cover artwork by Paskal Millet.
Finally many thanks to Sarah Vista and Clint Bradley for keeping the sound of the true west alive.
www.sarahvista.com
www.clintbradley.co.uk

Dedicated as always to I,P,F and the hounds.

As a boy,
I thought that life would be a long, exciting game,
But as a man,
I found it brought me nothing more than pain.

When you lose,
Each thing that warmed your soul with need,
Then you find,
Your temper frayed by others greed.

All alone,
I'm just a pawn in someone's game,
Dealing death,
For those who have no sense of shame.

On the trail,
The need for vengeance drives me far,
The blood will spill,
As I clutch another worn tin star.

You don't care if your morals are sold,
So let all of man's evil unfold,
In that search for those riches untold
... and Apache Gold.

CREDITS
Cover illustration: Paskal Millet
www.facebook.com/PaskalMilletArtwork
www.artstation.com/paskalmillet

You CAN teach an old dog new tricks

Danny DC   PjH

Steve & Ben Somers, KP, Dave W.

I

Douglas Fenraw could feel tight ropes cutting into his wrists and a boot heel on his neck, forcing his head against the rough floorboards of his cabin. Across the room he could see that his wife was struggling wildly to escape from the two bandits that were holding her down and roughly tearing at her clothes like coyotes.

His whole body tensed as he tried to free himself from his bonds but the owner of the boot only laughed and pushed down harder. Jessie Fenraw screamed out to her husband for help but that only served to arouse her leering attackers even more. Fenraw struggled again more fiercely and for one brief second the pressure eased until the boot crashed down on his head. His vision blurred and at first it was a warm and comforting feeling, like looking through a frosted window on a Winter's night, but a hot burst of pain followed which brought his vision back into focus. There was a piercing yell as one of his Jessie's attackers jumped back in agony. He could see his wife lying almost lifelessly on the floor with blood smeared thickly over her chin. Fenraw was drifting out of consciousness but praying that his son was still hidden in the bedroom. He cursed himself as the word 'Jimmy' fell from his lips. The thug standing over him muttered something and stormed into the next room. Fenraw heard a commotion, a youthful scream and a single gunshot.

As he awoke with a start, Fenraw could still hear the scream echoing across the valley. He was sitting bolt upright and his sweat-soaked clothes were clinging to him coldly. Even the blanket he had been sleeping on lay damp on the dusty ground. The fire was long dead and Fenraw felt only dread as he realised how long it would take before the sun once again brought some warmth to his bones. He reached for the half cup of cold coffee beside him and after picking out the dead flies that floated on its surface he gulped it down. As he packed up his meagre belongings he figured that it could never be too early to set off for Wilburg. Maybe there would be something in that town that could ease his nightmares. He yearned for a night's sleep that did not end in paralysing terror.

Guiding his horse around the base of the Gila mountains, Fenraw could see a speck of civilisation in the distance that he was sure was Wilburg. Further along the mountains he could see the beginnings of some type of industry; clouds of dust, wisps of black smoke and a shapeless mass of humanity toiling anonymously in the already punishing heat. His horse wheezed gently in the dusty atmosphere and Fenraw was glad that his torturous journey was nearly over. As he approached the town he struggled to see any signs of life but eventually noticed some figures shuffling around. No one acknowledged him as he rode straight through the centre of town. There was no welcome here for a sun-baked stranger and all eyes were fixed firmly to the ground in the hope that this was not another visitor who would bring some form of death and destruction to the community. It was too hot for grave digging or dodging bullets. Wilburg had only really sprung up when the copper mines outside town became established less than five years ago and Fenraw wondered how a town could look so jaded so quickly. Even the townsfolk looked worn out and beaten. The Blackwater Hotel was not hard to find in the barren town and when he reached his destination, Fenraw tied up his horse and removed his baggage and shotgun. He paused for a moment, took a long look around the town and exhaled a slow, grunt of disgust. Another dusty hell hole that stank of decay and desperation... if he was looking for a place to set him free from his troubled thoughts then this was not it.

The lobby of the Blackwater Hotel looked directly into the saloon and Fenraw immediately noticed some drunken old soaks hunched over tables clutching glasses of whisky. He placed his war bag on the floor close to the reception desk. Reception was perhaps a grand word for it as it was really no more than a rough wooden counter manned by a bored looking young girl who was combing her long, dark hair aimlessly.

'Mayor Cleets has booked a room for me,' said Fenraw quietly.

The girl put down her comb after a few more strokes at the locks then reached over to the selection of keys hung on nails on the wall behind her. She chose one and threw it down on the counter without making even an attempt at eye contact.

'Room 28'.

Before Fenraw could even pick up the key he heard a rasping voice behind him.

This gentleman won't be staying Laura Lee.'

Enraw turned around to face three leering roughnecks. He could tell right away from their worn clothes and dirty boots that they were no more than hired hands. Just a trio of red-faced drunks attempting to chase him out of town for nothing more than their next drink.

'I don't know who paid you,' said Fenraw calmly, 'But it's not worth it.' His arms hung loosely at his side and his empty palms faced the men.

'Kicking your hide has got to be worth it,' said the largest thug as he stumbled towards Fenraw with his knife drawn.

Fenraw let a length of heavy chain slide from under his coat sleeve. He gripped it tightly and whipped it into the face of his knife-wielding foe. The thug dropped to the floor clutching his bloodied face as the other two rummies stumbled a few steps back and went for their guns. Fenraw drew quicker and dispatched them with a shot each. The force of the close range blast flung them against the wall and two blood-splattered smears on the worn wallpaper tracked their progress as they slid lifelessly onto the dusty, wooden floorboards. The lead thug, blinded by blood, was scrabbling across the floor frantically reaching for a weapon. Fenraw kicked a gun towards his hand.

'Looking for that?' said Fenraw.

'I'll kill you, you bastard. I'll kill you,' yelled the man as he let loose every bullet in the pistol. The shots all went wild, splintering into the walls of the lobby, and as his gun clicked empty Fenraw finished off his would be assassin with a single bullet to the head.

'Room 28 you say?' said Fenraw picking his key off the blood-stained counter. The girl behind the desk was shaking with shock but managed to nod. He nodded down towards the lifeless bodies as he made his way up the stairs. 'You may want to get that cleared up before they start to smell.'

Wilburg's Council Chambers had a grand name but in reality it was no more than a two storey timber building five doors down from the worst saloon in town. It may not have looked much from the street but as Fenraw entered the lobby he was struck by the opulence within. A sweeping wooden staircase was the centrepiece of the room and it had been hand-carved and polished to perfection. Paintings in ornate, gilded frames covered the walls and a huge grandfather clock ticked with precision in the corner. Near the entrance a pretty, young woman greeted Fenraw from behind a small desk.

'Good morning Mr Fenraw,' she said. 'I understand you are here to see the Mayor.'

'That's right darlin.'

'If you take a seat I will see if he is ready.'

Fenraw dropped into a well-upholstered chair and lit a small cheroot as he marvelled once again at the majestic interior of the building. Before he had exhaled his first puff of smoke the young woman appeared from the double doors at the top of the staircase.

'Mayor Cleets and the council will see you now Mr Fenraw,' she piped and motioned towards the entrance.

Even as he climbed the stairs, Fenraw could see that the Mayor's office was even more grand than the foyer. The room radiated with the light from three huge chandeliers that almost dwarfed the room. Every surface, ornament and piece of furniture in the room was decorated with gilded metal or polished wood and each chair was upholstered in the finest leather. As Fenraw entered the office a small, painfully thin old man with white whiskers leapt from his seat and moved towards him offering a handshake.

'Jacob Cleets is the name. Sure am glad to meet you Mr Fenraw. Or may I call you Douglas?'

'Fenraw is fine.'

'Well Fenraw it is. Welcome to Wilburg. I assume you've already seen the rest of the town?'

'Sure Mayor. Some of the local boys said hello at the Blackwater.'

'Oh well, I... yeh, I heard. Nothing to worry about,' said Cleets as he adjusted his thick spectacles a little then looked towards the floor. 'Just a few cowpokes letting off a little steam.'

'Not a welcoming committee?'

Cleets laughed a little and retreated behind a huge oak desk that dwarfed him.

'Oh, no, no. I'm sure most of the townsfolk are pleased to see you. Specially as you are to be the law around here.'

Fenraw muttered something quietly and chose a seat close to the fireplace that gave him a clear view of the group and the door.

'Anyway Mr Fenraw, I would like you to meet the Wilburg town council.' Cleets motioned towards the other figures in the room who sat at the other side of the desk. 'Nate Rogers, Jed Ryker and William Stephenson.'

In stark contrast to their wiry leader, the trio were all portly and busting out of their $40 suits. Rogers in particular had an avaricious look and almost glittered due to the heavy gold watch chain, cuff links and other jewellery which adorned him.

'We got a problem Mr Fenraw. A big problem that only a man like you can sort out,' said Cleets. 'You do come highly recommended.'

Fenraw remained silent but Cleets continued anyway.

'We have an opportunity here Mr Fenraw. An opportunity to build more schools and churches and make Wilburg an important part of the civilised West.'

Cleets seemed to pause as if expecting some kind of response but Fenraw said nothing. Eventually Jed Ryker tired of the silence and addressed Fenraw directly.

'We have reason to believe that there is a sizeable seam of gold at a location in the Gila mountains a little over eighteen miles from town. We mean to mine that gold Mr Fenraw but some damn Apaches won't let us near it.'

'Gold? On their land?' said Fenraw.

'The West is changing Fenraw,' said Cleets. 'Those savages have no need for gold.'

'But the land is theirs?'

'By tradition maybe but not by law. Not anymore.' Cleets seemed to be losing patience a little. 'Mr Fenraw you seem a very blunt man, may I be forthright with you?'

Fenraw grunted.

'The town council of Wilburg are more than happy to find another location for the Chokonen Apaches if they move away peacefully. The whole venture will benefit them too.'

'So where are you going to put them?' asked Fenraw.

Nate Rogers finally piped up. 'We thought that yellow snake canyon would suit their needs.'

Fenraw let out a sharp, sarcastic laugh. He knew that that part of the country was an inhospitable stretch of scrub with no redeeming features. Even the vultures had a hard time surviving there.

'Think of the gold Fenraw. Think of the good it will do the town,' said Stephenson.

Fenraw immediately wondered how much of the wealth generated by the gold would even reach the people of the town. Would it put a roof on a new school or just put another fancy suit on these damn council members?

'Think of the good it will do you,' said Cleets. 'This could be a grubby task Fenraw but a well paid one.'

Fenraw said nothing but Cleets suspected he had taken the bait. 'If you help to move along the Chokonen I can personally guarantee you a job for life in Wilburg and a healthy wage.'

'What about a bonus?' asked Fenraw.

'Just let those miners do their job safely Fenraw and I'll make sure you get a handsome cut of the gold. A handsome cut.'

Fenraw paused in thought. He hated the greedy gleam in each councillor's piggy eye as they awaited his response. He feasted on the tension in the room as they all peered at him expectantly. Somebody was going to get paid for this damned dirty job and it might as well be him.

'It can't hurt for me to take a look out there,' he said eventually.

'That's my boy,' whooped Cleets.

The sweaty-faced councillors looked sickeningly smug with themselves.

I've got a few boys ready to ride with you Mr Fenraw, said Cleets. 'A lively bunch. Not afraid of a little Apache resistance and ready to do your bidding. They should be in the Blackwater about now.'

As Fenraw got up to leave, Cleets stepped forward and shook his hand vigorously as he pressed a dull Sheriff's star into his palm.

You won't regret this son.' Fenraw headed for the door and tipped his hat grudgingly at the council members. As he walked down the grand staircase a burning feeling of disgust was building in his stomach.

Mulligan's saloon lurked at the end of Wilburg's main street like a rotting tooth. Its mud-stained floorboards creaked under the weight of every crook, desperado and foul-tempered horse thief that passed through town. For four of Wilburg's least reputable townsfolk it was the ideal place to end a long day of extortion and bullying. As they strode into the bar it was empty apart from a few deadbeat gamblers and a solitary figure at the back of the cavernous room with his large-brimmed hat pulled low over his eyes. The man sat quietly almost hugging what little shadow there was in the room. His black clothing and footwear had been fancy at some point in the dim past but now they were worn almost to the point of extinction and permanently scarred with dust from the trail. Half a glass of whiskey sat on the table in front of him but even his motionless state still caught the attention of one of the thugs. Eavis Carter was the type of mean bastard who would probably have carried out paid dirty work just for the satisfaction of a job well done because whatever money he did make went swiftly on liquor and whores. Before he had even ordered a drink the pot-bellied giant laughed, mumbled something to the rest of his friends and swaggered over to the stranger's table.

'Hey saddle tramp,' yelled Carter as he kicked the stranger on the boot. 'Why the hell you stinking up this joint when you ain't even drinking?' Carter stuck two dirty fingers in the stranger's glass then sucked the whiskey off them. 'This damn hooch has been sitting on the table since before we got here.'

The stranger said nothing and did not even lift his head to face the glaring roughneck. The stranger's indifference drove Carter into an instant fury and with a firm slap of his hand, he knocked the man's hat right off his head and onto the floor. The man only moved his head slightly and levelled his eyes to meet Carter's.

'Ain't you got nothing to say you silent son of a bitch?' spat Carter.

The stranger's legs kicked out from beneath the table making full contact with Carter's shins and sending him crashing forward onto the table. With a swift move the man picked up the whiskey glass and smashed it onto Carter's head. Stunned, Carter fell backwards onto the floor but he regained his balance and leapt back quickly with a roar, blood blinding him and waving his pistol at his attacker. A single shot cracked through both the table and Carter's jaw. The thug fell to the floor but his screams were masked behind a gurgle of blood, broken teeth and bone.

The stranger lifted his smoking gun from beneath the table and stared at Carter's amigos. The one that drew his gun was dead before his pistol left its holster and the other two dragged Carter quickly through the saloon doors. The remaining patrons turned their attentions swiftly back to their game and stared at their cards intently. The barman's son was dispatched to get the undertaker as the stranger picked up his hat and sat back down.

Fenraw had barely settled in at Wilburg's dilapidated jailhouse when a small boy banged on the door frantically and alerted him to the bloodshed at Mulligan's. Fenraw sighed as he rose from behind the woodworm infested hunk of timber that passed for his desk and pinned the tarnished star onto his waistcoat. He checked his gun and moved the heavy chain in his coat sleeve into position. As he strolled to the end of the street he knew he was being watched.

Old Mulligan himself was mopping up blood when Fenraw entered the saloon.

'Nothing for you here Sheriff,' said the ancient barkeep. 'Just a little misunderstanding. Nothing more.'

Fenraw smirked as he followed the blood-stained track which led to the body of Carter's associate which was dumped unceremoniously behind the bar.

'Just a misunderstanding, eh?' said Fenraw as he nodded in the direction of the corpse.

'Self defence Sheriff,' said Mulligan, 'Just self defence.'

Fenraw looked at the hopeless drunks who were staring at their drinks.

'Anybody here see anything?' The staring continued. 'Now there's a surprise,' said Fenraw as he walked towards the drifter. The man looked familiar but Fenraw had seen so many saddle tramps that they all began to look the same. The table with the single bullet hole was back in place and the man was once again sheltering under the brow of his hat.

'Get up,' said Fenraw. 'I've had too shitty a day to even wonder what when on here. You can spend the night in jail and we can piece this whole sorry story together tomorrow.'

The man did not move or even acknowledge Fenraw. With a sigh of resignation, Fenraw drew his pistol quickly and pressed it against the man's head.

'I'm in no mood to shoot the breeze with some dirty drifter so you had better get your ass out of that chair and head for the jailhouse or I'm going to deliver some summary justice right now,' said Fenraw quietly. His prisoner stood up and lifted his hands into the air slowly. Fenraw took his gun and pushed him towards the saloon door.

With the killer from Mulligan's under lock and key, Fenraw stepped out onto the porch of his new Sheriff's office. Since arriving in Wilburg he had dealt with three assassins, those grasping councillors and a mute murderer already. He was not sure who he hated the most and it was not even sundown yet. He realised he had to see what kind of help Cleets had lined up for him before he really knew how deep the shit he was in really was.

Fenraw walked back through the lobby of the Blackwater to get to the saloon. He noticed that a half-hearted attempt had been made to mop up the blood of his welcoming committee but the floor boards and rug were still marked with dirty crimson patches. Fenraw had low expectations for the posse assigned to him and he was not disappointed. Propping up the bar were ten mercenaries that looked as if they had been kicked out of hell. Almost to a man they were grizzled, red-eyed thugs. Their clothing was worn and dirty but their guns and knives were gleaming. Each man was fully armed and sporting the tools of their trade openly.

A couple of them were more smartly dressed than the others. One sported the type of garish, well tailored suit favoured by big time gamblers and his thick hair was immaculately oiled down. The dandy stepped forward as soon as Fenraw entered the room.

'Why Mr Fenraw, so pleased to meet you,' said the man offering a handshake. 'I'm James Canton. I've been appointed by the good fathers of this town to assist you with our little problem out of town.'

Fenraw kept his hands to himself and nodded towards the rabble, 'Is this it?'

'Why yes Mr Fenraw, ten good men, straight and true. Let me introduce Mr Frederic Dodge, Clancy Averill, Billy State...'

'I don't need to know their names,' interrupted Fenraw. 'I just need to know that they will be ready to ride out in a couple of days.'

'Of course Mr Fenraw. We are here to be at your service. Won't you join us for a drink?'

'I don't think so,' said Fenraw as he cast his eyes over the group and they stared sullenly back at him,

'Perhaps I could organise a little warmth from a good woman,' said Canton. 'You look as if your journey has been a little arduous.'

'Just have them ready to go when I say,' Fenraw sneered.

'I certainly will Mr Fenraw, I certainly will,' said Canton remaining defiantly pleasant.

Casting his eye over the rabble once more, Fenraw turned away and headed back to the jailhouse in a foul mood.

Fenraw's prisoner was sitting in exactly the same position in his cell when he returned. As he threw himself into the chair behind his desk Fenraw let out a deep sigh. They both sat motionless for a while until Fenraw started to look through the drawers of the old desk in front of him. He laughed sarcastically as he pulled two rusted Deputy badges out and threw them on the desktop. Any papers he found were thrown into the fireplace then finally he discovered half a bottle of whisky. He pulled out the cork and was about to take a drink but he paused before placing the bottle back down. Fenraw looked at the whisky then he looked at the drifter, staring into the distance.

'Do you want it?' he shouted over.

The man nodded so Fenraw walked over to the cell and pushed the bottle through the bars. The mute gulped down the rotgut frantically.

'Whoa,' said Fenraw. 'Take it easy. Give that back you greedy bastard.' The man did as he was told but the bottle was almost empty. 'Jesus Christ. A man that drinks like that ain't going to be around for too long.' Fenraw gripped the bottle like a weapon and rested his shoulder on the bars of the cell. 'Listen friend. This silent act is beginning to wear a little thin. I need to find out what happened at Mulligans. You'd better tell me something or I'm going to have to start looking at ways to make you talk.'

The man stared at the floor for a moment then opened his mouth wide and pointed inside. Fenraw looked closely into the chasm and saw that he had no tongue, just a small stump of red flesh where it should be.

'What the hell happened there?' asked Fenraw. 'Apaches?'

Silent only shrugged.

'Maybe I'm thinking this is what's behind the bloodshed at Mulligan's,' said Fenraw. 'Maybe those roughnecks were ragging on you and things got a little out of hand?'

The man had returned to his motionless state.

Fenraw kicked the cell door furiously, 'Godammit, you better give me something boy or you will be swinging on a rope by dawn. Give me something, you are all I have got. One of your friends is halfway to hell now. It was self defence wasn't it?'

The man nodded.

Fenraw calmed down a little and went back to his chair. 'Just as I thought.

Some local cowpokes ragging on a mute.' Fenraw picked up a Deputy badge and began to pick at the rust with his thumbnail.

'You seemed to take care of them pretty well though Mr Silent. One in the undertakers, three skipping town and not a mark on yourself. All that blood as well.' Fenraw put the whisky back in the drawer. 'Having seen my latest crop of recruits maybe I could do with a little assistance of my own. Someone who could watch my back when I'm leading out Canton's thugs against the Apaches.' Fenraw could see that Silent was listening. 'Are you looking for a job?'

Silent stood up and nodded.

Fenraw thought for a moment then he got to his feet and lifted the jail cell keys from a hook on the wall behind him.

'Let's get you tidied up then friend. Welcome to Wilburg's law enforcement.'

Fenraw tossed the deputy badge straight through the bars of the cell and Silent caught it first time.

III

Being a black lawman in a place like Benton, Arizona was never going to be easy, as memories of the civil war were still festering like an open sore, It had never been easy for Fred Kelly since the day he was born and it certainly did not look as if it was going to get any easier today. He was trapped in his own jailhouse with his brothers Jim and George. Their prisoner, Darius Schaeffer, was in a cell behind them and his family of inbred misfits were trying to secure his release with a hail of lead.

'Goddamn Schaeffer,' yelled Fred as another shotgun blast turned a section of the jailhouse door into splinters. 'Those crazy bastards are going to kill us all, including you.'

Schaeffer giggled wildly from his shelter under the cell's bunk. 'They want you dead far more than they want me free you black devil.'

'We should shoot him now,' yelled George as he reloaded his Colt. 'This family of killers just ain't going to stop.'

More bullets peppered the walls of the jailhouse and another shotgun blast blew out an entire window frame.

'I don't know how many of them are out there Fred but we are running out of bullets,' said Jim.

Darius overhead the conversation and leapt out from his cover screaming.

'They are out of ammo boys, come and get me pa.'

'Jesus Christ,' shouted Fred as he leapt forward and jammed his rifle butt through the bars onto Darius' face. The prisoner slumped to the ground but Fred had broken his cover and a bullet whistled over his shoulder. Splinters from the wall behind him dug into his back and he fell to the floor with a yell.

'Fred? Are you hit?' shouted Jim.

'It's just a cut.' Fred lifted his hand from his shoulder and it was dripping with blood. The shooting intensified. Bullets began to ricochet off the cell bars and every piece of furniture was being reduced to sawdust.

'We've got to make a move,' hissed George from behind clenched teeth.

'I told you we should never have taken this shit job,' said Jim. 'Goddamn, I don't want to die in Arizona.'

'Well we can die behind this furniture or die out on the street,' said Fred.

'Let's take it to them.'

'Damn right,' said Jim.

George loaded the final two shells into his shotgun and yelled, 'Let's do this.'

The brothers took their positions. Fred stood at the side of a bullet scarred door while Jim and George took a window each. They paused for a moment then moved into position and blasted every shot they had into the street. When the smoke cleared all of the Schaeffers were dead in the dust.

'Well I'll be,' said Jim. 'Looks like we had enough ammo to do the job.'

'Not quite,' said a voice from the other side of the street. The Kelly brothers span round and aimed their empty weapons instinctively at the stranger.

'I think you will find at least four shot from behind,' said Fenraw as he broke cover from behind a water butt.

Fred Kelly looked at him and a broad smile broke over his face, 'Oh shit! Good to see you Douglas. Nice timing. How the hell did you find us here?'

'You're not a hard man to find,' said Fenraw as he walked over and shook Fred's hand firmly. 'Looks like another bit of trouble I've saved your ass from.'

'No, no,' beamed Fred. 'We were doing just fine.'

Fenraw pointed at the bullet-ridden jailhouse. 'It certainly looks that way.'

'Do you mind?' George said to his eldest brother. 'Who the fuck is this?'

'An old friend of mine. Don't you remember I told you I rode out with Douglas Fenraw back when you were still scratching your ass in short pants.'

'What? The mercenary?' said Jim.

'No. Not the mercenary,' growled Fred. 'Me and Mr Fenraw were gainfully employed in evicting illegal settlers from those mines in the north of New Mexico.'

'You mean kicking out those prospectors to make way for company men,' said George moodily as he began picking weapons from the dead bodies in front of him.

Fred's mood darkened as he glared at his sibling. 'I told you never to mention that bullshit again brother.'

'Hey,' said Fenraw attempting to lighten the atmosphere, 'Maybe we could go inside what is left of your office and talk things over.'

Fred was glaring at George but addressing Fenraw. 'Maybe that's a good idea.'

As they all walked back inside the jailhouse, Darius had gained consciousness and began yelling at the Kellys.

'Why the hell are you black devils still alive? What happened to my kin?'

'They are all gone you crazy fool,' said Jim. 'It's over.'

'Satan. Satan,' babbled Darius. 'You are all in league with Satan. I curse thee black devils...'

'Shut the hell up,' shouted Fred as he jammed his rifle butt through the cell bars and silenced Darius once again.

'Is he behind all this?' said Fenraw.

'Damn right,' said George. 'He's ready to swing for attacking three local women but the judges are taking so long to pass sentence that his whole family got wind of where he was holed up.'

'Is he going to prison?'

'No, he cut them all up pretty good,' replied Fred. 'Near killed them. I can't see anything but the rope for him.'

Fred pointed towards a chair and he and Fenraw sat down at the bullet-ridden desk. As he opened a drawer, Fred giggled and pulled out a bottle of whisky with a flourish.

'The gods must be smiling down on me,' he grinned. 'All those bullets and they didn't hit my hooch.'

'So how did you get involved keeping the law here in Benton?' said Fenraw.

Fred paused as he poured out the liquor into four dusty glasses.

'The good folks of Coolridge just could not get used to a black sheriff so we had to leave town real quick and move down the road to here.'

'So is this town any better?'

'Not a damn bit. They were happy enough for us to take on the job but when they heard that the Schaeffers were coming to town they disappeared like ghosts.' Fred jerked his thumb at Darius, 'As soon as we deal with him I reckon we are moving on again.'

'How about coming back to Wilburg with me,' said Fenraw. 'It's only about a day's ride North. I've got a little work out near a goldmine.'

Fred seemed interested almost immediately, 'Gold, eh?'

'It's on Apache land but I've been asked to secure it for some Scottish miners that the town's Mayor has duped into working for him.'

'Apaches?' said Jim. 'And four of us?'

'I've got nearly a dozen other hands but I trust them less than the Apaches.'

'Sounds like a suicide mission,' said George.

'Yes it does,' said Fred. 'But it sure beats staying in this ghost town.'

'The job stinks Fred but there could be a little gold for ourselves in it. Enough to get us out of trying to keep the peace in these damned dirty towns forever.'

'You planning to take a little for yourself Douglas?' asked Fred.

Fenraw sat on the edge of what was left of a desk and crossed his arms. 'I've seen where the money is going and I don't like it.'

George and Jim looked at their brother for a response. Fred began to load the weapons on his desk into a leather roll. For a few moments he was deep in thought then he stood up sharply.

'Benton can go to hell. Let's get mining.'

Fenraw strode forward and shook Fred's hand firmly. 'I can't say you won't regret it my friend but if you are still alive in a few weeks you will be a richer man.'

Fred reached into a desk drawer for a few items then slammed it shut. 'Jim. George. Gather up all the weapons and throw them on the horses.'

'What about him?' said Fenraw, pointing at the unconscious Darius in the jail cell. Fred picked up one of the Schaeffer's pistols, fired four shots into the prisoner and threw the gun to the floor.

'He got killed in the gunfight. Tragic.'

IV

When Fenraw rode back into town with the Kellys beside him it did not go unnoticed. When people saw that the brothers were sporting deputy badges word spread around Wilburg at a rapid rate. Jim Canton, Clancy Averill and Frederic Dodge were sitting around a table at the Blackwater when the news reached them and it pushed Dodge into a frenzy.

'Damn that Fenraw,' he roared and pounded the table with his fist. 'First he brings that mute fool into the posse then three slaves. How many people does he need to clear out those fucking Apaches?'

'Steady yourself Mr Dodge,' said Canton in a measured tone.

'To hell with steady,' yelled Dodge. 'We don't need all these people. We get out there, kill the savages and take whatever gold they have. Why the hell should we share it out even more with Fenraw's hired hands. I thought Cleets hired us to help him out?'

'He did my friend,' said Canton calmly. 'But he also gave Mr Fenraw the autonomy to bring on board who he sees fit.'

Dodge was bemused. 'What the hell does that mean?'

'The Mayor lets Fenraw hire however many guns that he wants Frederic,' said Averill. He tapped one of Dodge's clenched fists with a long bony figure and smiled broadly. 'Maybe he just don't trust us.'

'Maybe so but I ain't working with no blacks. Fenraw can go to hell.' Dodge slammed his empty glass on the table then yelled at the barman. 'What the hell have I got to do to get a drink round here.'

Canton quickly grabbed an empty bottle from the table and banged its base firmly down on Dodge's hand. Dodge let out a yell and a curse as Canton leaned forward menacingly.

'Might I remind you Mr Dodge that you need to moderate both your tone and your volume less the good folks of Wilburg go running to Sheriff Fenraw and inform him of your intentions.'

'If Fenraw knew of our intentions he would have us swinging on a rope right now,' said Dodge quietly as he nursed his hand.

'Mr Dodge may be putting his point across in a rather uncouth manner,' said Averill. 'But it is a point nonetheless Jim. Are we to share our gold with an ever increasing band of Fenraw's followers?'

'Those Kelly boys are old acquaintances of Fenraw but God knows why he gave the mute a badge,' said Canton. 'Maybe that black-hearted swine has finally seen the light and now he is doing God's charitable work.'

'I find that hard to believe,' smirked Averill.

'Either way Clancy, when we get the gold I am not sure Mr Fenraw and his friends will be around to collect their share.'

Fenraw had not expected a warm welcome in Wilburg but most of the townsfolk seemed too preoccupied to care. Although the population looked fairly grim most of the time anyway, there was now a palpable aura of fear across the whole town. Fenraw could feel the unease as he rode into town. The poker-faced Mayor Cleets was already waiting outside the locked doors of the jailhouse.

'Goddamn,' yelled Cleets. 'Where in the hell have you been Fenraw?'

'Recruiting,' replied Fenraw sternly.

The Mayor looked at the Kelly Brothers as if they were shit on his shoe then turned back to Fenraw. 'I thought I gave you all the help you needed.'

Fenraw laughed sarcastically. 'Those cutthroats? I need some real help I can rely on. These are the men and there is another one waiting.'

'That mute killer? The damn fool is in there right now. He won't even open the door.'

'Maybe he doesn't want to talk,' smirked Fenraw.

'Is that supposed to be funny? You've got the manpower now you need to get your ass moving out to the O'Brien place west of the mines.'

'Those homesteaders that have been supplying food to the miners?' said Fenraw.

'Hell, they won't be supplying anything now. The Chokonen attacked them last night.' Cleets dropped down onto a chair on the porch, exhausted by his own yelling. 'They killed them all Fenraw. Women, children... everyone.'

'How do you know?' said Fenraw.

'One of those Scotsmen from the mine went to pick up some supplies. He noticed some buzzards circling and when he got to their place it was a blood bath,' said Cleets quietly.

'Those Apaches can be savage alright,' agreed Fred.

Cleets ignored him and continued with his news. 'Bodies spread across the ground, cut up real bad. It's ungodly. You've got to see it Fenraw. See what you are up against and deal with it. The people around here are scared real good. A bloodthirsty attack so close to town does not go unnoticed.'

'Seems like you are doing all you can to spread the news Cleets. Nobody actually saw the Apaches right?' said Fenraw as he got off his horse.

'Dammit Fenraw. Who else could it have been?'

Fenraw walked over to the jailhouse and unlocked the door as the Kelly brothers dismounted and loosened their saddle bags. 'I'll check it out.'

'When Mr Fenraw? When?' croaked Cleets. 'I want swift retribution. I want the Chokonen to know that attacking white folks will not be tolerated.'

The Kellys were glowering at the old man but Fenraw ushered them inside. As Fenraw stood in the doorway he glared at the Mayor.

'You had better watch how you talk to my friends Cleets,' he said quietly. 'I'll ride out later and check out the O'Brien ranch.'

Cleets winced as Fenraw slammed the door in his face.

Fenraw did not want to be seen dancing to the Mayor's tune but he was keen to find out exactly what had happened at the scene of the massacre. The shades in the jailhouse were down and Silent sat in an empty cell with the door open.

'You work here now you crazy bastard,' said Fenraw as he shook his head in disbelief. 'You can sit at the desk.' He turned to the Jim Kelly who stood close to a window. 'Let some light in for mercy's sake, it's like a damn undertakers in here.

Jim pulled open a set of dusty drapes and the sun flooded in. It did the room no favours and only helped to highlight Silent's bedraggled state as he walked from the cell and sat next to the rifle cabinet..

'This well-attired gentleman is Mr Silent, our latest associate,' Fenraw said to the Kellys sarcastically.

'God damn Fenraw,' whistled Fred. 'Only the best for you, eh?'

Fenraw moved over to Silent and patted him firmly on the shoulder. A small cloud of dust rose up around his hand.

'He might look much but he is a very capable man,' said Fenraw. 'Mr Silent these are my very good friends the Kelly brothers and I'm sure we are all going to get along just fine.' Silent nodded at the Kellys as the very slightest of smiles danced across his lips.

'But first we have got to get you looking your best,' continued Fenraw as he opened an old wooden chest near the corner of the room.' He pulled some clothing out and threw it over to Silent. 'These were left behind by the last occupants. They may have a few bullet-holes and blood-stains but they are better than those damn rags you have on.'

With Silent clad in an ill-fitting but slightly smarter set of duds, Fenraw's posse all loaded their horses with guns and ammunition and picked up the rest of the group at the Blackwater Hotel. It was a motley crew with the dandy pairing of Canton and Averill alongside Dodge and a seven other lowlifes, like two whoremasters leading a jailbreak. Unsurprisingly, Dodge and many of Canton's other men were furious at the sight of the Kellys and Silent riding upfront with Fenraw but they kept their comments to themselves as they rode out of town.

Canton himself was as belligerently cheerful as ever as he brought his horse alongside Fenraw. 'Why good afternoon Mr Fenraw. So nice to see you back again. And your new friends are?'

Fenraw kept looking at the trail ahead but he grudgingly answered Canton. 'This is Fred, Jim and George. You may have already met Silent.'

Canton spoke loudly and slowly to Silent. 'How are you my friend.'

'He's not deaf,' shouted Fenraw.

Silent only scowled.

'Well it's nice to meet you all. Let's hope we live long enough to enjoy a drink together back at Wilburg.' Canton pulled his horse back and rejoined his gang behind Fenraw.

'That damned snake,' spat Fred Kelly furiously. 'How the hell did you get involved with those wild dogs?'

'They came with the job,' answered Fenraw. 'Now keep riding.'

'Are you sure about them?' asked Fred.

'Not in the least but we might have some trouble up this trail so maybe we need some cannon fodder. If things get rough let them crazy bastards ride into it first.'

'Hell, I'm more worried about them than the Apaches,' said Jim casting a wary glance back at Canton's mob.

'Keep your eyes on all of them,' said Fenraw, then they rode on silently.

After a few hours small wisps of smoke were visible from the McNairn's mines. Fenraw whistled and signalled to everyone to head in that direction. Canton brought his horse alongside them immediately grinning broadly. 'Nice day for a raid on the Apaches. Eh, Mr Fenraw?'

'We are just seeing where we are with the Chokonen Canton. It's not a slaughter.'

'Maybe some of those miners could be persuaded to join us though Douglas,' Canton continued. 'If it is going to get them closer to the gold, who knows?'

'We've got all the help we need,' snarled Fenraw.

'Just a thought Mr Fenraw. Just a thought. If we get a few of those immigrants alongside us we could end this today.'

'We're all immigrants here Canton,' Fred Kelly shouted over.

'Some more than others Mr Kelly,' said Canton smiling as he reigned in his horse and dropped back once again.

Although the miner's camp was visible first by some plumes of smoke as the posse from Wilburg rode on some shacks, piles of rubble and discarded wooden beams came into view at the base of the mountain. A large, timber house sat right in the middle of the settlement and its simple grandeur was in stark contrast to the dusty surroundings. The McNairns knew they were coming. Every miner was waiting around the camp and a small group stood defiantly on the front porch steps of the house. As soon as the posse were within earshot Billy McNairn stepped forward. The mine boss was a small and swarthy character with a balding head but bushy, flame-red whiskers. His pants and workshirt were ingrained with dust and sweat patches seeped through his clothing.

'That's far enough friends.'

McNairn was unarmed but the clutch of men directly behind him had rifles and the other miners spread across the site were clutching tools and thick sticks as weapons.

'What are you after?' McNairn continued.

'Just passing through on our way to the O'Brien place,' said Fenraw.

'You don't pass through here to get to the O'Brien's and there ain't nobody over there to speak to no more,' growled McNairn as he narrowed his eyes against the slowly sinking sun.

'I know,' replied Fenraw bluntly. 'We're on our way to see what went on over there. Just thought we would check and see if things were OK here.'

'Checking we are still fit enough to dig, eh?' asked McNairn.

Fenraw was getting a little annoyed at the miner's argumentative tone but he tried to hold back his fury.

'I'm Douglas Fenraw. The new law in Wilburg.'

'I know who you are,' shouted McNairn. 'You are Cleets' hired gun. Looking to slaughter the Chokonen and move us on to Apache land to mine.'

Fenraw snapped and started yelling. 'I don't give a good goddamn what you think Mr. I want to know what went on at the O'Brien place and no more. Just thought we would check that you hadn't all been skinned and burned alive here but hell, I think we have wasted the best part of a day on you ungrateful sons of bitches.'

McNairn was small but his muscular frame was twitching as he yelled back at Fenraw. 'Then get the hell off our land. Damned mercenaries.'

Fenraw grabbed his heavy chain from his saddlebag and jumped off his horse in one swift move. Canton's gang could sense the scent of violence and grasped their weapons with glee as the miners moved forward. It took a woman's voice to prick the tension.

'Now William that's not how we usually treat our visitors, is it?' All eyes fell upon the woman who had appeared at the door of the cabin. She was clad in worn denims and a collarless shirt but her shapely figure filled the plain garb well. In a camp where everything was dusty brown her long, glossy black hair and full, red lips shone out like a beacon. She was no maid but undoubtedly a full-bodied, mature woman. 'Won't you take a drink Mr...?'

'Fenraw'.

'We haven't been introduced Mr Fenraw. I'm Nancy McNairn. Sister-in-law to Billy here and surrogate mother to these drifters.' She waved her hand in an affectionate flourish towards the mine workers. 'Come over and sit with us.'

'We ain't staying,' snarled Fenraw.

Nancy ignored his indifference and continued. 'Well let me bring a little spring water to you and your friends.' She reached inside the cabin and brought out two large jugs of clear water. As she moved towards the Wilburg posse all eyes followed her and Canton's dogs licked their lips with avarice. Fenraw's men held out their cupped hands for Nancy to fill. They drank what they could gulp down then wiped their wet hands on their dusty faces. McNairn's men stood silently, still tensed for battle, but the strangers were too busy leering at Nancy to notice their aggressive stance.

Canton smiled broadly at Nancy and tipped his hat. 'So nice to see such a beautiful desert flower out here in all this scrub.'

Nancy ignored him and moved to offer Dodge some water but he was reaching towards her in a lecherous fashion.

'Maybe she's a mirage Clancy. I reckon I'd better take a feel.'

Nancy had a knife out and placed against Dodge's crotch before his fingers could make contact.

'How about a feel of this blade,' she hissed. 'Don't ever try to touch me you flea-bitten dog or I'll cut you in two.' Dodge gasped and moved back in his saddle slowly.

Fenraw suppressed a smirk but then anger filled his head once again.

'Goddamn savages,' he yelled as he climbed back onto his horse. 'We've wasted enough time here. You're on your own McNairn.' Fenraw paused slightly as he looked over at Nancy then he dug his heels into his horse and rode off. The posse followed leaving the McNairns and the miners in a cloud of dust. McNairn watched them go as everyone but Nancy drifted back to work.

'God-dammit,' spat McNairn. 'Everywhere we go there is someone ready to mess things up.' Nancy stepped closer and put a comforting hand on his shoulder.

'There's nowhere left to go now Billy,' she said quietly.

McNairn kicked a small rock angrily and peered at Fenraw's posse who were now no more than a speck in the distance.

'Your damn right Nancy, there ain't a bastard alive that can move us now.'

After a few more hours in the saddle the O'Brien's ranch appeared on the horizon. Without saying a word the Wilburg posse slowed their horses a little in unison. Since leaving the mine there had not been a lot of talk but all Fenraw could really hear was some muttering about "that damned woman". He felt a twinge of some kind of emotion when he thought back to Nancy's feisty behaviour. It was a feeling he had not felt for some time and he immediately banished it to the back of his mind.

'There it is,' said Fred Kelly as he nodded towards the ranch. 'Looks pretty quiet now.'

'The dead don't tend to make much noise brother,' shouted Jim.

Fred kicked his horse gently and moved up alongside Fenraw near the front of the pack.

'What in the hell do you think of those miners Douglas?'

Fenraw only grunted and peered at the hills behind the O'Brien house as he rode on.

'Hell they should be glad we even checked to see if they were alive,' continued Fred.

Silent was some way ahead of everyone else and suddenly he pulled up his horse sharply and raised his arm in the air to halt the rest of the group. He pointed to some scrub less than ten feet away. A pair of legs, clad in blood-splattered pants, could be spotted sticking lifelessly out from behind a bush.

Silent leapt from his horse and made his way over to the body.

'Take it easy there friend,' Fenraw shouted over to him.

Silent looked at the body for a moment then reached down and dragged the figure from the undergrowth. The corpse was a middle-aged man and his throat had been cut wide open. What had been a bloodstain from his collar to the top of his boots had dried a dirty brown and the buzzards had begun to make a meal of his eyes and lips. Fenraw and the Kellys winced a little but some of Canton's thugs almost whooped with delight.

'Damn savages. Injuns. I told you,' grinned Dodge.

'What do you think now Fenraw?' yelled Clancy Averill.

'Just keep riding,' said Fenraw as he motioned to Silent to get back on his horse. They rode on but every twenty yards or so another lifeless body came into view, each more butchered than the last. Outside the house were dark patches of dried blood in the dust and all over the porch. The axes, knives and clubs that had been used in the massacre lay discarded on the ground and bullet holes riddled the front of the house.

As they all dismounted Canton strode over to Fenraw, seemingly unmoved by the slaughter.

'What's the next move Mr Fenraw?' he said with a grin. 'A violent act of this magnitude cannot go unpunished.'

Fenraw glared deeply into Canton's eyes and spoke quietly out of everyone else's earshot. 'Whoever did this is going to die... very soon.'

Canton seemed a little uneasy at Fenraw's intensity but did not let that get in the way of his constant need to chatter.

'I don't think there is a whoever Douglas. The bloodlust. The cruelty. It is plainly an Apache attack. Those godless heathens know no boundaries to their savagery, we have to act.' Although Canton was addressing Fenraw he was obviously playing to the crowd and his words garnered a few yells of support from his cronies.

Fenraw turned his back on Canton and strode towards the house. Silent followed him but Fenraw signalled to him to wait outside. The front door was now no more than a couple of rusted hinges. Across the parlour were blood stains and they all seemed to lead to a room at the back. Fenraw reached a closed door. Before he opened it he thought he could feel a dull ache like a boot heel was pressing down on his neck. Although the sun was dropping he felt hot and clammy. Thoughts of his wife and son filled his mind and his chest started to tighten. He shook the dark thoughts away. A slight breeze was wafting a foul smell around his nostrils as he opened the door. It was where the women and children's bodies had been dumped.

Outside, the posse were kicking their heels in the dust. Silent stood motionless on the porch.

'What in the hell is he doing in there?' said Averill.

'Probably checking the dead for gold teeth,' grunted Dodge.

Fred Kelly spun round and grabbed Dodge by the throat.

'Why you dirty son of a bitch...'

Their disagreement was brought to a halt as Fenraw burst out of the house and strode towards his horse. His face was white with rage.

'Damned Apaches,' he yelled. 'Let's kill them all.'

Over ten miles away from the O'Brien place Fenraw was still riding like a demon, pushing his horse forward so hard that specks of sweat were drifting off the beast on to Silent and the Kellys who were riding close by. Canton's men were struggling to keep up but eager not to miss any bloodshed. Fred Kelly pushed his horse alongside Fenraw's.

'These damned Chokonen have faced American troops dead in the eye,' Fred shouted over. 'Do you think our posse of flea-bitten marauders are going to scare them?'

'Flea-bitten? Speak for yourself,' said Jim Kelly attempting to lighten the mood.

Fenraw rode straight ahead, glaring at the dark hills that were looming towards them.

'You go back if you want,' he shouted above the rattle of hooves on dust. 'Someone's got to pay.'

A small patch of dried-out woodland was before them and as they approached a gap between the trees Fred galloped ahead again then pulled his horse to a halt across the track. The rest of the riders stopped abruptly.

'What in the hell are you doing dumb ass,' shrieked Dodge.

Fenraw was furious. 'Get out of the way Kelly.'

'Douglas we need to think this through,' said Fred. 'What is your plan? Storm into some Chokonen camp at nightfall? We've got less than an hour of daylight and we don't know where they are or how many are out there?'

'Losing your nerve boy?' said Averill. Canton's men roared with laughter.

Fred ignored them and continued to reason with Fenraw. 'Please, think about it Douglas. Let's set up camp and send out a couple of scouts. Once we know what we are up against we can ride over there at daybreak and slaughter them all. Hell, I don't care but going there now is suicide.'

'Them Indians ain't nothing,' piped up Dodge. 'Let's get the job done and get the hell back to Wilburg.'

'I'm afraid I have to agree with our friend here,' said Canton. Kelly looked shocked at his unexpected ally. 'There is more to be gained with a little caution in this case,' continued Canton.

Fenraw was still glaring into the distance but he eventually realised that the entire group were waiting on some response. He was about to let loose a sigh but he checked himself and remained emotionless. 'We'll ride ahead a mile or so and look for a camp. Silent and I will scout ahead for tomorrow.'

'Jesus H. Christ,' wailed Dodge. 'When are we going to spill some blood.'

'Shut your damn mouth,' barked Fenraw as he rode on.

Nancy McNairn slammed a pot of hot coffee down on the kitchen table.

'I just don't think it's right Bill,' she said. 'You let them ride out there when you know that was no Apache attack.'

Billy McNairn sat at the table, staring at his empty plate.

'I don't know nothing,' he growled.

'You know, damn you. Black Bob the trapper told you there were no Indians near the O'Brien's place. He saw a posse heading East that night and they weren't no fucking Chokonen.'

'He couldn't see nothing in the dark,' said Billy.

Nancy was furious and laid her hand on the pot by mistake.

'Oh, Jesus,' she cursed and wrapped a rag around her scalded fingers. 'That's bullshit Bill,' she continued. 'And now you've let those men ride straight to their deaths.'

Billy could not look Nancy straight in the eye. 'Damned mercenaries. They don't deserve nothing better. The Mayor's hired flunkies, that's all they are. Hired to kill Apaches. Hell, if they could mine the gold themselves they would probably kill us too.'

'And what if they rile up Teboca? The Chokonen will ride through us to get to Wilburg. I thought you were getting somewhere with them?'

'You can't reason with no damn Apaches,' said Billy.

'Well it sure in hell beats fighting them.' Nancy turned away from Billy in disgust and stared out the window at the miners working. 'Poor fools. There is no more than thirty of them out there. Bob was sure there was near a hundred Chokonen around that camp.'

'That old fool has been out in the sticks too long,' said Billy sarcastically.

'He's no fool,' said Nancy. 'When Fenraw and his boys reach them it will be a massacre. They will be lucky to get away alive.'

Billy grinned darkly. 'If they do reach the Chokonen camp there will be nothing left of them, just a dirty stain in the dust.'

As darkness fell the Wilburg posse set up camp in a little patch of bushes close to a river. Averill and Canton set up a small fire to brew some coffee but the rest of the thugs slurped on bottles of whisky from their saddlebags, working themselves into an even more murderous rage. Fred Kelly and Fenraw walked over to the river to fill their canteens.

'I ain't got a good feeling about this Douglas,' said Fred.

'We've seen worse,' replied Fenraw as he stared back in disgust at Canton's howling mob.

'Do you trust them?' asked Fred.

'Do I hell. That's why I've got you and your brothers. I'm not even sure about Silent yet.'

'Where the hell did you dig him up?'

Fenraw took a swig of water and stared over at Silent who was sitting close to his horse away from the rest, clutching his gun and peering into the darkness.

'There's something familiar about him,' Fenraw said quietly. 'Anyway, he's got no love for Canton and his men so that makes him the nearest thing we've got to an ally. I'll take him out tonight. Get his measure. But if he makes any wrong moves you put a bullet in him just like the rest.'

Fred laughed a little. 'I'd like to put a bullet in everyone of them right now.'

'You stick with me friend and you might just get that chance,' said Fenraw. Fenraw and Kelly secured their canteens and walked back to Canton and the others who were slouched around a camp fire. Fenraw crouched down and flicked a small pebble into the flames before he spoke.

'We've got fifteen men, almost double that in guns and whatever else you've got for killing. We take that to the Chokonen camp. Whoever is left standing shares whatever guns or gold that we find.'

'And that's the plan?' asked Averill incredulously.

'Pretty much.'

'So what about the camp's survivors?'

Fenraw paused then stared directly at Averill. 'We don't leave any.'

'Now that's a plan,' cackled Canton.

'Yeh', said Dodge. 'Let god sort them out. Those weasels would leave us dead in a ditch. No question.'

Averill looked furious but said nothing.

'What about the cotton boys?' said Dodge as he waved a finger dismissively at the Kellys.

Fenraw breathed deeply before answering. 'They're with me.'

'Does that sit right with you Dodge?' asked Canton.

'No slave is getting a cent of my share,' Dodge mumbled to Averill.

Fenraw leapt at Dodge and kicked him off the small log he was perched on.

In a single move he pinned Dodge's shoulders to the ground with his knees and pulled his knife from its sheath. He dug the tip of the heavy blade into the skin at the top of Dodge's ear and sliced upwards leaving a one inch tear. Fenraw muffled Dodge's scream by pressing his free hand over his victim's mouth. Canton's gang leapt up and drew their weapons. Silent and the Kellys already had theirs drawn.

'Hold on now Mr Fenraw,' said Canton calmly even though a flicker of terror danced across his eyes. 'You touch one of my boys like that and I'm liable to put a bullet through your head.'

Fenraw ignored Canton and stared at Dodge as he spoke. 'I would trust any of them with my back before you, you piece of horse shit. They are with me so you had better get used to it.'

Canton was starting to get twitchy.

'That's fine Douglas,' he shouted. 'But you had better move clear right now or you won't live to see another Apache.'

Fenraw paused, still staring at Dodge and refusing to acknowledge Canton. His knuckles were white as he gripped the handle of his knife then slowly got to his feet and walked towards the Kellys and Silent.

Dodge clasped his ear and let out a long, slow scream. Canton signalled to his boys to holster their weapons. They all did reluctantly and a couple of them helped Dodge to his feet.

'Easy now Mr Dodge,' said Canton as he led Fenraw's victim away from the fire. 'Let's get this ear patched up.'

'I'll kill him Jim,' spat Dodge. 'I'll kill that bastard.'

'Yes, yes Frederic,' Canton whispered soothingly. 'Just wait till we get to the Choko camp my friend. Then we'll kill them all.'

VI

An uneasy atmosphere had settled over the camp as Fenraw and Silent rode out. Dodge was still nursing his bloodied ear and mutinous rumblings emanated from Canton's gang. No one had the nerve to say anything to Fenraw though and Canton himself was just as annoyingly jovial as he always was. Fenraw felt as if he was leaving the Kellys behind in the lion's den but he knew they could take care of themselves. Besides, if they did not get an idea of what they were about to face then their attack would be nothing but a suicide mission. As they trotted quietly through the dark, Fenraw began to question himself about seeking vengeance on the Chokonen but the memories of what he had seen at the O'Brien place spurred him on.

After only travelling a half mile or so, Fenraw was already vigilant for any signs of life. He suspected he was only a few miles from the Apache camp and he was sure that they may have scouts on patrol, expecting reprisals for the massacre. Although darkness had fallen, the moon was bright and it illuminated the surrounding countryside. If anything appeared on the horizon he was sure he would notice but he also realised that Silent and himself were in plain view. Fenraw gestured to his partner and they headed towards a small, wooded area for cover.

They rode side by side through a rough track in the woods and Fenraw noticed that Silent was peering ahead, scanning behind every bush and tree.

'Sure glad I brought you along for the conversation,' Fenraw said quietly.

Silent smiled a little but kept his attention on the road ahead.

'I reckon I'd get more sense out of you than that fool Dodge.'

Silent scowled and made a violent, slashing motion with his thumbnail across his throat.

'Well, you never know my friend. Mr Dodge might force our hand before too long.'

With his free hand, Silent patted the large knife which he stored in his boot. Fenraw knew he wouldn't have to ask twice if Dodge had to meet his maker.

'Y'know I was thinking...' Fenraw's words froze in the night air as Silent raised his arm quickly and pulled up his horse. A massive felled tree blocked their way and its sharp, dead branches jutted into the darkness. Fenraw heard a loud click behind them and cursed under his breath silently, knowing he had let his guard slip.

'Get off those damn horses and turn around real slow,' came a voice out of the darkness.

Fenraw and Silent did as they were told. A wild bearded figure clad in a patchwork of animal furs stood before them clasping a Spencer shotgun. He swayed the gun gently, covering them both, but Fenraw knew that was unnecessary. Both barrels unleashed from this range could put them both in the grave. He had seen a Spencer reduce a man's arm to a bloody stump once in a pointless gun fight in a bar near Los Lunas.

'Bit far from home aren't you partner?' said Fenraw. 'Must be slim pickings out there for you.'

'There is more than pelts that interest me,' replied the stranger. 'I don't intend to end my days hunting rabbits and bears.'

'Maybe your days will end a little sooner than you think my friend. Especially if you keep holding folks up in the woods.'

'Shut your damn mouth,' barked the stranger. 'Throw your guns down, right in front of me. Do it.'

Fenraw and Silent placed their rifles on the ground slowly, keeping their eyes on the mountain man's trigger finger all the time.

'And the pistols. Don't take me for no damn fool.'

As they placed their guns down Fenraw prayed that Silent would not make a move.

Fenraw could sense from the man's relatively calm demeanour that there could be more guns out there pointed straight at them. The mountain man seemed to know that if he only hit one of them the other would not be a threat. Suddenly Silent leapt straight at the stranger with no regard for his own safety. He moved swiftly and managed to push the barrel of the shotgun into the air as the mountain man tightened his finger on the trigger. The wild vibrations of the shot pulsed through Silent's arm but he continued his attack regardless, forcing the stranger to the ground and pounding his face with his other fist. Before Fenraw could even move another shot rang out from the dark just as he had expected. A misty spray of blood burst from Silent's back and the power of the shot made his body spin as if in some gruesome ballet. He fell into a bush where he lay lifeless. Fenraw stood still waiting for the next shot then he heard more movement in the bushes behind him. He felt a dull thud on his neck and saw that familiar flash of light once more before darkness enveloped him.

As Fenraw struggled to open his eyes, a sharp, stabbing pain filled his head. He tried to pull himself up immediately but his body felt as if he was being held to the ground by lead weights. He gradually focused his eyes and could finally make out the mountain man who had held them up. His face was covered with blood and he was kicking Silent's prone body where it lay in the bush. Two other equally wild looking characters were beside him. Although they too were clothed in a patchwork of furs one was huge and broad while the other was small and painfully thin. All of them had that tanned, leathery skin that came with spending a lifetime outdoors and masses of hair sprang from every visible part of their body.

'Leave him dammit, he's dead,' said the small one spoke in a croaking voice. 'Look the other one is rousing.'

The stranger was unwilling to give up. 'Where's my gun? I'll take his damn head off.'

The large wild man spoke at last. 'What? And let every damn Indian and roughneck round here know where we are? That first shot was enough to land us in deep shit as it is.'

The stranger went to land another kick at Silent but with one firm push from his beefy hand his large accomplice sent him crashing to the ground again.

'How you feeling friend?' said the small man to Fenraw with a malicious tone.

Fenraw's mouth was dry but he managed to spit out some words.

'Just fine you hairy bastard.'

The small mountain man gave Fenraw a swift kick in the jaw and the foul taste of blood filled his mouth as he fell back onto the ground.

'We want to know what brings you here partner,' said the little man. 'And you had best give us some answers unless you want to be in the same state as your friend over here.'

Fenraw raised his head slightly and spat on the ground.

'He won't say nothing,' said the stranger as he continued to wipe the blood off his face. 'I should have shot them before they got off their horses.'

'No need for that Clem,' said the man mountain. 'We don't see many folks round these parts. Maybe we can show this fella a bit of a good time.'

Clem stared angrily at his hulking partner.

'We ain't got time for that Ned. You'll need to find someone else to play with.'

The hairy giant moved towards Fenraw with a disturbing leer plastered across his face. 'No, no. There's time enough.'

Suddenly Ned's eyes opened wide and he took a deep, gasping breath before falling forwards like a toppled pine. Fenraw managed to roll out of the way through that sheer burst of adrenalin that comes when facing sudden death. As the huge figure crashed to the ground Fenraw noticed Silent's boot knife jammed to the hilt between Ned's shoulder blades. Before Clem could tighten his finger around the trigger of his shotgun Silent emerged from the shadows swinging a log that mate full contact with the top of Clem's head. The trapper fell lifelessly to the ground and Silent immediately started to wrestle the shotgun from his grip. The small mountain man placed his rifle quickly on the ground and raised his hands in surrender.

'Now listen... these fellas here made me...' he pleaded.

Silent unloaded both barrels into the small man's chest and the force propelled the trapper off his feet completely and into the same bushes were Silent himself had lay. Fenraw blinked as specks of blood covered his face. Silent stood still, scanning the three bodies for any signs of life.

'That certainly was some resurrection,' said Fenraw when he had recovered his breath. 'What does it take to kill you friend.'

Silent helped Fenraw to his feet.

Fenraw regained his balance then looked closely at the badly ripped and bloody cloth around Silent's shoulder. 'Just a flesh wound I take it?' he said in disbelief. 'Playing possum were you? You took a damn beating, that's for sure.'

Silent only nodded then moved towards where the horses had ran to while Fenraw looked over the bodies of the mountain men.

'Don't suppose these damned trappers have anything worth taking apart from their guns,' he shouted over to Silent. 'Might as well take them,' he murmured to himself. 'Those darn shots have probably woken up the entire Chokonen nation. Let's take a look.'

As the day's first beams of light changed the sky from black to dark blue Canton's gang were awake and ready to ride out. Their desire for violence was so strong that they had barely slept. Fenraw took a little longer to come to his senses. They were too close to the Chokonen to risk lighting another campfire and his body was so cold that he felt he was in the grave already. Just like every day he had a few seconds as he opened his eyes when his mind was at peace but as he fully regained consciousness dark thoughts flooded in once again. His burning desire for vengeance against the Chokonen had tempered though and the hate he felt when he rode out from the O'Brien place had subsided. For a moment he had his doubts but to back down in front of Canton's jackals was an even more unsavoury thought. Silent appeared by his side, offered him a hand and helped pull Fenraw to his feet.

'You ready for this friend,' said Fenraw quietly as he looked at the rough patch on Silent's back. 'Is your shoulder okay?'

Silent nodded and gently tapped the pistol in his holster.

'Do you think we are doing the right thing?'

Silent only shrugged.

'Hell, we are doing it anyway,' said Fenraw as he brushed the dried dirt off his pants. He slapped Silent on the back and pushed him lightly towards the rest of the group who were already waiting. They took their place alongside the Kellys, a division so clear it looked like two posses fixing to fight each other.

'Nice to see you have finally woken Mr Fenraw', said Canton.

'We've got plenty of time Canton,' barked Fenraw. 'You'll get your share of killing soon enough.'

'Just keen to complete our piece of the business Douglas, that's all.'

Fenraw ignored Canton and addressed the group.

'The Chokonen camp is about eight miles from here. On our approach we'll have cover from a small hill.' He motioned towards Silent. 'That's where we took a look last night after meeting our trapper friends.'

'Sounds like they wanted to turn you out like a two dollar whore', cackled Dodge.

Fenraw ignored the mocking laughter of Canton's rowdies.

'They may have a watch up there now but Silent will deal with them. Once we reach the top of the hill we'll be view for sure so we haul ass down into the camp and hit them hard.'

Dodge and a few of his oafs whooped in anticipation.

Fenraw stared at them hard.

'This is just a warning to them that any act of violence similar to what happened at the O'Brien place will not go unanswered. This is not a slaughter.'

'That's not what you damn well said last night,' said Dodge.

Fenraw ignored the comment. 'If we linger too long and they get time to get organised it could be our heads on a stick. It's a fairly large camp so be warned. Leave the women and children alone whenever possible.'

Dodge spat in the dust contemptuously.

'Very fine words,' shouted Averill. 'But can we get a damn move on?'

Fenraw looked at him sullenly. 'Let's move out.'

The posse reached the bottom of the hill as the sun was beginning to appear over the horizon. Fenraw, Silent and the Kellys were leading the group once again. As their horses started up the incline Fred Kelly drew his horse closer to Fenraw.

'Hellfire, a daylight raid on an Apache camp?' he said quietly. 'I'd have been safer back in Benton.'

'Yeh?' said Fenraw with a grimace. 'But you wouldn't be having as much fun.'

'Maybe you are right,' Fred said with an uneasy grin. 'But then again...' Fred's words trailed off as they reached the brow of the hill and the full size of the Chokonen camp became apparent. 'Oh shit,' he gasped.

Fenraw motioned to the rest of the posse to ride up the ridge quickly.

'You want some bloodshed?' he shouted. 'Well here it is.' Fenraw spurred his horse towards the camp and the rest followed.

For a tribe so aware of their surroundings, the Chokonen seemed to have no idea of the impending attack. The first few braves that peered from their tepees to investigate the sound of rumbling hooves were met with a hail of bullets. The shots and the screams of a few women who were preparing a campfire soon roused the rest of the Apaches. Despite Fenraw's warning, Canton's men took great pleasure in cutting down the squaws and their slain bodies fell onto the fresh flames.

Fenraw noticed the atrocity immediately but he was too busy putting a bullet in every new Apache that appeared in front of him. For every Chokonen whose body hit the dust three more would appear. The Kellys and Silent were also emptying every bullet they had into the crowd but the Chokonen's response was rapid. A single rifle shot rang out and it lifted the top of the skull from one of Canton's grinning thugs. A spray of red decorated the sky and the still-leering bandit dropped from his horse. The thud as the corpse hit the ground was drowned out by a battery of Apache gunfire. Five more of Canton's men and as many horses met their maker in an instant. Jim Kelly's elbow was reduced to a bloody mess and a bullet ripped into Fenraw's thigh. The sharp, hot pain cleared Fenraw's head in an instant and he knew that another volley of shots like that would finish them all.

'Jesus H. Christ,' he shouted as he turned his horse around. 'Move out goddammit, move out.'

Canton, Dodge and Averill were already on their way but Silent continued to push forward into the camp with an almost suicidal zeal.

'Silent, get the hell out,' yelled Fenraw.

'Leave him Douglas,' shouted Fred Kelly. 'You're hit bad. Looks like he's fixing to die anyway.'

Silent was hitting an Apache with every bullet but too many were approaching him.

'God damn crazy mute,' said Fenraw as he wiped a splash of blood from his eye and spurred his horse towards Silent.

'Fenraw you damn fool,' cursed Fred and turned to his brothers. 'George. Get Jim back to town and don't stop till you're there.'

'Jesus Christ Fred, we ain't getting paid enough for this shit,' shouted George.

'I've pulled Fenraw out of worse hell than this,' said Fred and charged forward.

With Silent, Fenraw and Kelly still shooting wildly the Chokonen fell into positions of cover around the centre of their camp and it gave Fenraw just enough time to pull his horse in front of Silent. Fenraw's eyes were burning with fury as he stared directly at his deputy.

'I said get the hell out,' he yelled.

A bullet passed through the top of Fenraw's shoulder and he gasped in pain. The sight of fresh blood seemed to snap Silent out of his killing frenzy.

'We have got to go now!' screamed Fred. 'I ain't dying before I get some gold.'

The Chokonen were well placed to pick off the intruders now so Fenraw, Kelly and Silent kept their heads down, turned their steeds around and headed towards the base of the hill. They could defend no more and escape was their only option. Six Chokonen followed them on horseback and they let off another volley of gunfire. Fred's horse caught the worst of the shots and it slumped to a halt throwing him violently across the sharp, stony ground. Silent pulled up his steed and jumped off. As his feet hit the ground he fired six shots at the Apaches and each bullet hit Chokonen flesh. Fenraw had also stopped and as he aimed rifle shots at their pursuers who were still advancing, Silent pulled Fred onto the back of his horse.

'Go, dammit, go,' ordered Fenraw.

As Silent's horse moved up the hill they were an open target. Fenraw reloaded his rifle and laid down some covering fire to protect them. The first wave of Chokonen on horseback were soon slaughtered but more were appearing in the distance. With each shot he fired, Fenraw could hear less and less noise. The pain in his shoulder and thigh felt almost warm and comforting. He was thinking of the faces of the Chokonen. He could see their fury and sheer desire to kill his posse but he could also see surprise. Surprise, as if they had no damn idea why they were being attacked.

'Douglas, get up here.' Fred's yell brought Fenraw's concentration back into focus and the pain in his body was sharp once more.

Fred and Silent had made it to the top of the ridge but more Apaches were bearing down on Fenraw as they navigated past the braves and horses that had been slain. Fenraw turned and started his ascent. He held his rifle by his side and dug his heels into his horse's ribs. The horse moved up the hill at a pace but Fenraw knew he was an open target. Strangely he felt a wave of calm but also a sense of inevitability. As the shots rang out he held on hard to his horse and smirked to himself. Hell, another Apache bullet won't make no difference. He felt a bizarre wave of joy tingle across his body and dampen the fierce pain in his wounds. Jessie. Jimmy. I'm coming home. Bullets whistled past him but the cloak of death never fell as he pushed forward mindlessly.

VII

Fenraw sat at the heavy oak table in the kitchen of the McNairn place, nursing a cup of steaming coffee in his hands. The smell was strong and pure, far from the burned out brew he usually made for himself. Nancy was tidying around the kitchen but achieving very little as if she was unwilling to take the weight off her feet.

Fenraw broke the silence. 'Living up here with all these men. The talk must get pretty rowdy.'

'It's nothing I haven't heard before Mr Fenraw,' said Nancy. 'There's little room for god-fearing talk round here where your days could end right now with an Apache's bullet or under a ton of rubble.'

'Why don't you sit down?'

'I'll sit down when I'm damn well ready,' replied Nancy.

Fenraw raised his eyebrows and took a deep draught from his cup. The warm brew spread a satisfying tingle across his chest. Nancy continued to tidy but eventually she threw down her dishrag and dropped into a chair across from Fenraw.

'How are your wounds?' said Nancy.

'Just another ache now,' said Fenraw. 'It was worth it for the bullets.'

Nancy sighed as she looked at the two glistening slugs on the table.

'Gold bullets?' she sneered. 'We are killing ourselves for copper and they've got gold to spare. They must be pulling it out of the ground with their hands.'

'You will be mining it soon if Cleets has his way.'

'But how many of us will have to die before that happens? How many dead Apaches will it take to allow us to get on with our job?' said Nancy.

Fenraw admired the slight blush on her cheeks and the burning indignation in her eyes. He glimpsed the firm shape of her bosom beneath the rough plaid shirt then tore his gaze away sharply.

'Does it bother you?'

'Yes it bothers me Mr Fenraw. Not because I'm a woman. I'll shoot those savages myself if they threaten my family but I've seen too many die already just to get here.' Nancy seemed annoyed that she had let her defences slip.

'Was it a hard road to Arizona?' said Fenraw.

Nancy sighed as she reached for her empty cup.

'From getting on the boat at Southampton to getting here it has been nothing but death. My husband Stuart and I left Scotland for a new future together, away from the misery. The mining work at home was hard and cold but our men were skilled. Some businessman from London promised us a new life over here. Easy mining and riches. Thirty of us landed in California two years ago and only eighteen of us made it here. Had to do our own share of the killing along the way and when we got here there was nothing but a little more heat.'

Fenraw was not sure what to say but after a pause he pushed the gold bullets over the table to Nancy.

'Well there is a little gold to get you started.'

Nancy frowned then let out a sigh of resignation.

'Blood-stained bullets Mr Fenraw? You certainly know how to treat a woman.'

'Well you should have left them in him'. Billy McNairn appeared at the door of the kitchen. He glared at Fenraw with a fury.

'Billy McNairn. How dare you,' responded Nancy. 'I don't care if it's a bandit, Apache or any damn cowpoke that turns up here but I'm not going to let anyone bleed to death on our porch.'

'He wasn't on our damn porch,' yelled Billy. 'If that fool trapper hadn't brought him here he would be lying where he fell out in the scrub and wouldn't be our damn problem. Why did you come back here anyway Fenraw? I told you to stay away.'

'I wanted to warn you that the Chokonen might be restless.'

'Shit, they are restless now alright since you and your damn mercenaries riled them up. Hell, you've done more harm coming back here anyway.'

Fenraw said nothing and continued drinking his coffee.

Billy still had a lot on his mind. 'So where are the rest of those dogs?'

'I sent some back to town. Some ran back to town anyway but most of them are dead.'

'And you thought you would come back here to save us all,' sneered Billy. 'That's bullshit.'

Fenraw felt the acid sting of anger rising inside him but he breathed deeply and held it down.

'I know it wasn't the Chokonen that hit the O'Brien place,' he forced himself to say calmly.

'So now you know,' crowed Billy. 'Half your posse is dead and the Chokonen fixing to slaughter every white man around. Now you know. Well I'm glad you finally learned the truth. Now get the hell off my land.' Billy stormed out of the house, kicking the porch door as he went.

'Your brother-in-law don't seem too happy,' Fenraw smirked.

'It's not funny Mr Fenraw,' said Nancy as she slammed down the coffee pot she had been cradling onto the table inches from Fenraw's hand. 'These are working men here. They don't have the stomach for a war with the Apaches. God damn, ain't mining hard enough.'

Nancy looked out of the window into the distance and her shoulders seemed to droop in resignation. Fenraw instinctively felt that he should offer some consolation but every fibre in his body refused to accept the possibility of any human contact. The last woman he had ever held was Jessie as she slowly grew colder in his arms.

'I'll send some extra men from Wilburg,' he said. 'Just until this calms down.'

'It is not going to calm down Douglas,' replied Nancy. 'You've kicked the hornet's nest now.'

'Well that was nice,' said Fenraw.

Nancy was angry and confused. 'What was?'

'You called me Douglas.'

'Did you like that?' Nancy purred as her mood seemed to change in an instant as she walked slowly over to Fenraw.

'It makes a change,' he answered impassionedly.

Nancy arched her eyebrows and leaned over the table towards him.

'Was it a pleasant change?'

Fenraw could almost feel her warm breath and his eyes were fixed on her full, red lips.

'Yes it was', he whispered in anticipation. What he did not anticipate was the full slap across his jaw that nearly knocked him out of his chair. Nancy drew back her hand again but Fenraw grabbed her quickly by the wrist.

'God damn you hellcat,' he roared. Out of the corner of his eye he noticed Nancy's free hand reaching for the bread knife which lay on the table. Fenraw stood up swiftly and spun Nancy round so quickly that she skidded across the floorboards on her behind.

Before Nancy even got to her feet she was yelling. 'Get out of my house you heathen. My husband is barely in his grave and you think you can lay your hands on me. Billy was right. You're nothing but a dirty mercenary. I'm glad he didn't tell you who killed the O'Briens.'

Fenraw could feel shooting pains coursing through his body but his temper numbed them slightly.

'What do you mean you crazy witch? What did he find out?' He moved towards Nancy threateningly but she was lurching towards the door.

'You touch me again and I'll scream out to every man in this mine. There is no one out there with any love for you Fenraw. They'll bury you in a grave four hundred feet down.'

Fenraw knew he was in no position to take on anyone at the moment and Nancy could sense his resignation.

'Get out of here. Get out you dog and don't come back.'

Fenraw glared at her then reached for his jacket which was hanging behind a chair. He noticed that Nancy had patched over the bullet hole on the shoulder.

'Crazy bitch,' he hissed as he pushed past her at the door.

'Get out,' Nancy yelled and slammed the heavy door behind her. As she lay against it her body shook with anger and she noticed the blood-stained bullets. She grabbed the slugs then threw open the door once again and hurled them into the dust. 'Take your damned, dirty gold too,' she yelled at Fenraw but he was already gone.

Darkness had fallen on Wilburg and most of the townsfolk had settled down for the night. In contrast to the gentle glow of lamps coming from the homes of the citizens, light blazed from the windows of the council chambers. A meeting was in session and tempers were flaring. Jim Canton sat on a small chair in front of Mayor Cleets, Jed Ryker, Nate Rodgers and Will Stephenson who peered at him across the finely polished table. The air was thick with the smoke from expensive cigars and an empty whisky bottle stood next to some glasses.

'God damn Canton,' yelled Cleets. 'You mean to tell me you came back into town with two men?'

Unusually Canton was a little flustered. 'The three slaves and the mute were not far behind.'

'I don't give a good god damn about them Canton,' the Mayor roared in a voice that belied his small frame. 'Those are Fenraw's men, I don't care where they end up. I paid you to wipe out those Apaches.'

'That was the deal Canton,' drawled Will Stephenson as he puffed a fat cigar.

'But you made Fenraw lead the party,' protested Canton weakly.

'Bullshit,' said Nate Rogers. 'You knew the arrangement.'

Although Canton was a strapping individual he was belittled by the group of men glaring at him over the table. Although they were either too fat, too weak or too old to match him physically they towered over him with their intellect and wealth. He knew that to disagree with them could lead to a visit in the night from an unknown assailant. They could afford the finest killers, even ones more ruthless than himself.

'There were too many Apaches,' stuttered Canton. 'It was suicide.'

'But you followed that Fenraw right into the belly of the beast?' said Ryker. 'Are you right in the head boy?'

'He was riled up Mr Ryker. The massacre at the O'Briens' place... it inflamed him.'

'Well that's fine,' said Cleets angrily. 'But you should have come back to town for some reinforcements, not followed that mad fool.'

'Didn't you get no help from those damn miners?' said Stephenson as he puffed his cheroot calmly.

Canton paused for a moment as if he was weighing up whether to give the councillors the full story but his tired brain could barely function.

'The miners knew that the O'Briens weren't hit by no Apaches.'

'Jesus Christ,' wailed Cleets. 'How the hell did they find out?'

'I think they saw something,' said Canton while staring at the door.

'Saw what, you donkey's ass?' Cleets was purple with fury and banged his bony fist on the table.

'I don't know,' answered Canton sheepishly.

'You don't know?' said Ryker. 'What part of kill them all and stay unseen don't you understand?'

Stephenson stubbed his cigar into a thick, glass ashtray.

'Mr Canton. I think you may need to step outside for a moment. You have placed us in a very disadvantageous position.'

He's placed us in a pile of steaming crap,' said Cleets bitterly. 'We don't need to confer gentlemen.' He reached into his drawer, pulled out a large wad of notes and hurled the bundle at Canton. 'Get your ass in gear Jim. I want you to hire as many men as you can muster and have them ready to go back to that Chokonen camp when I say so. Young, old, broke or just stupid. I don't care but I want an army ready to ride.'

'What about Fenraw?' said Canton as he stuffed the cash into his coat pocket then leapt from his chair.

'I'll deal with fucking Fenraw,' growled Cleets. 'Now get the hell out!'

It was early evening as Fenraw rode back into Wilburg. Usually at this time of the day there were signs of life around town but today it was eerily still. As he tied his horse to the post outside the jailhouse he heard the click of weapons being loaded inside.

'Fred? Jim? It's Douglas,' he shouted out before approaching the door.

The door opened slightly and Fred peered out. When he noticed that Fenraw was alone he opened the door fully.

'Douglas, how are you doing my friend?' he said quietly.

'What's going on?' said Fenraw. 'Is Jim okay?'

Jim was laid out in the bed of one of the cells and his wound had been hurriedly dressed.

'I'm fine brother,' he shouted over. 'But for how long I don't know.'

'What do you mean?' said Fenraw as he shut the door behind him.

'That damn doctor couldn't get out of here quick enough,' said George Kelly. 'Seems that we are about as popular in this town as fleas on a dog.'

Fred and George were sat at the desk with an array of weapons close by. Silent sat on the bed of the other cell staring into space.

'What have you heard?' said Fenraw.

'We're not sure Douglas,' answered Fred. 'But that doctor was mighty shifty. Scared too. It looked like he was expecting a volley of gunfire through the window at any moment.'

'I reckon Canton's high-tailed it back to town with a story about something other than the truth about what happened out at the Chokonen camp,' said George.

'He made it back, huh,' said Fenraw.

'I saw him late last night Douglas,' said Fred. 'I shouted out to him in the street but he ran over to the chambers like a scared rabbit.'

'Probably to get his version of events over to Cleets before you came back,' said George.

Fenraw sighed deeply as he placed his pistol, rifle and chain on a table close to the cells. 'I'll see to Cleets but not now. I'm too damn beat.'

Fenraw dropped down into his seat behind the desk and exhaled deeply. Everyone in the room was still for a few moments until Fred broke the silence

'How did you get on at the McNairn's place? Looks like they patched you up pretty good.'

'Damn ingrates,' spat Fenraw. 'They didn't want no help. In fact they've got us down as starting an Apache uprising.'

Jim Kelly propped himself up in bed and winced a little as he put some pressure on his bandaged elbow.

'Looks like she's got real healing powers Douglas,' he leered. 'Did she give you a little extra soothing on the side?'

'Crazy bitch,' said Fenraw. 'She nearly took my eye out with a knife.'

'Nice,' said Jim with a smile. 'Fiery. My kind of woman.'

'We won't be back there anyway,' said Fenraw. 'Ungrateful bastards. Let them rot.'

Fred Kelly walked over to the window. 'Jesus. Is there anywhere in this state where we ain't pariahs?'

Jim laughed a little. 'Hell, not for a few hundred miles around at least.'

Fenraw walked into the cell and sat in a chair opposite Silent. 'How you doing friend?'

Silent nodded and sighed a little.

'No new bullet holes?' said Fenraw as he leant forward and pulled at Silent's buckskin jacket. 'You're a lucky man. So close to all those Apaches? Things got a little intense there, eh?'

Silent nodded again and looked at the floor.

Fenraw drew his chair a little closer and lowered his voice. 'I'm not sure that you were bothered either way if you came back here.' Silent's head stayed down but Fenraw tapped his knuckles under Silent's chin until he nudged his head up to make eye contact. Fenraw stared at him intently.

'I don't want you dead in the first trouble we come across. We've got a long way to go, I need you alive. Let some of Canton's fools lead the charge. This whole thing is just about gold. I don't want us all dead just to line Cleet's damn pockets with money. You hear me?'

A flicker of a smile passed over Silent's face as he nodded in agreement.

'Good,' said Fenraw as he pulled Silent to his feet roughly. 'Now get off that damn bed. I'll need some shut eye before I face those snakes at the council chambers.'

It was late in the following morning when Fenraw was woken from his dark slumber by a weak tapping on the jailhouse door. His sleep had been deep and muggy but had inevitably ended in terror and cold sweat as the noise aroused him. A ray of pale sunlight from the small cell window temporarily blinded him as he pulled himself off the bunk and sharp pains emanated from his thigh and shoulder. The tapping continued. Fenraw looked around the jail and saw that everyone else was sleeping. The Kellys lay close to the desk under horse blankets and Silent was sitting at rest in the corner, eyes closed but still clutching his rifle.

'Jesus,' growled Fenraw. 'Don't no one else hear that door.'

A few bodies stirred but nobody woke. Fenraw focused his bleary eyes on the clock. He had slept for damn near fourteen hours.

'Okay, okay. I'm coming,' he shouted hoarsely as he made his way to the door. 'This better be damn important.'

He looked out of the window before unbolting the door. Mayor Cleets' secretary stood on the porch with a plain look of distaste on her face.

'Now there's a pleasant sight for my tired eyes,' said Fenraw has he stared at her intently.

The secretary looked at Fenraw as if he was something nasty that she had just scraped off her boot.

'Mayor Cleets would like to see you as soon as possible Mr Fenraw.' She said his name as if it was bile in her throat.

Fenraw looked up and down the street but could see little sign of life. The secretary looked uneasy standing in front of Fenraw but she waited for some confirmation. Fenraw made her wait.

'You tell Mayor Cleets I will be along directly darlin'.'

The secretary shuffled off towards the council chambers and Fenraw closed and bolted the door.

'Wake up you lazy bastards,' he shouted. 'I've got a meeting with the Pope of Wilburg.'

A long row of Wilburg's menfolk stood in a ragged line outside an old stable block behind the Blackwater Hotel. Inside, behind a rough, wooden bench sat Canton, Averill and Dodge. Canton and Averill had regained their composure somewhat, and after a bathe and some fresh clothes they looked as dandy as ever. Dodge looked much worse. His face was unshaven, his clothes dirty and a blood-stained bandaged was strapped around his head and over his ear. Canton and Averill sipped on freshly brewed tea, Dodge slurped down the Blackwater's lowest grade whisky.

Canton gestured to a young man standing by the window.

'Stop ogling those damn citizens and open the door boy,' he yelled.

As the doors were pushed open the men shuffled into the room a few at a time.

'Let's have an orderly queue gentlemen,' said Averill loudly. 'This is important business we have here not some cattle show.' He pointed to a spot in front of the table. 'Come on now, start the line right here.'

An ugly and unkempt brute presented himself at the front and stepped forward. Averill's face was a picture of disgust.

'Why I know this here fella,' Canton cackled. 'He's a good ole boy and no mistake. Why I seen him slug down four fools at once in a brawl at Mulligan's. We got to get him on board.'

'Any friend of yours Frederic,' said Canton with a slight sigh.

Averill gripped Canton's arm a little and whispered to him. 'Is this really all we are looking for Jim. Roughnecks?'

Dodge was glaring at Averill but unsure of what he had said.

'Clancy, let's take what we can get right now,' said Canton equally quietly. 'This is a big ole job. We are bound to need a few men to eh... lead from the front, if you get my drift.'

Averill's haughty contempt was etched across his face but he sat back in his seat and said nothing.

'Welcome to Wilburg's new law enforcement friend,' said Canton as he stuck out his hand to the filthy recruit. 'Any friend of Frederic here just has to be of good stock. Take your first payment from Mr Dodge here and wait in the bar for further orders.'

The man moved down the table a little and another prospective lawman moved forward. This specimen was no more than five feet tall and not a garment on his body was of the correct fit. He had just about enough teeth to hold a cigar and lurking beneath his mop of unkempt hair were two boss eyes peering in different directions.

'Jesus Christ,' hissed Averill in a stage whisper.

Canton ignored his associate's dissent and smiled broadly at the young man.

'Good morning fine fellow,' he beamed. 'Would you like to join us in our quest to protect this fine town?'

'I sure would,' muttered the youth.

'Do you have any skills that would benefit a keeper of the law?'

'I got a shotgun,' said the young man after some thought.

'Well, that would come in handy,' said Canton, winking at Dodge. 'Any other talents?'

'I've worked killing pigs over at the Johnson place.'

'Well you never know when that may come in handy friend,' Canton smirked. 'Welcome to the group.'

Averill pushed back his chair and flounced out of the room in disgust.

'Looks like it's down to you and me Dodge,' said Canton with amusement. 'Next.'

Fenraw wondered where all the menfolk of Wilburg were at this time of the day but did not ponder too long. His body hurt like hell and he could feel the bile rising in his throat at the thought of further dealings with the town council. He also felt a little hollow in the pit of his stomach every time he thought of Nancy McNairn and in the odd moments between pain and anger that is where his mind took him.

'Crazy hellcat,' he hissed under his breath as he threw open the door of the council chambers.

The rapid movement startled Cleets' secretary.

'Why Mr Fenraw... if you would...' she stuttered.

'I know where I'm going sweetheart,' said Fenraw and immediately made his way up the stairs.

When Fenraw strode into Cleets office he was surprised to find the old man on his own. The Mayor was unmoved by Fenraw's sudden arrival and barely looked up from his desk.

'Take a seat Mr Fenraw, I will be with you in a minute.'

To hell with that,' roared Fenraw as he moved towards the desk and glowered down at the old man. 'What's going on in this town? What kind of bullshit stories did Canton come back with ahead of us?'

Cleets remained calm. 'Please take a seat, we're not animals.' Cleets placed his engraved gold pen lightly on the desk and looked up from his documents. 'You see Mr Fenraw, this is just another example of behaviour that I have to question as it is not what I would expect from a man of the law. Bursting in here, making demands. I must admit that recently I have had reason to ask myself why I hired you.'

'Why did you hire me? To start an Indian war? To run the McNairns off their land? Jesus H. Christ the trouble round here don't extend to no more than bar fights and a bit of rustling. What do you need me for?'

Cleets peered at Fenraw over the thin rim of his round spectacles.

'As I remember Mr Fenraw, your main task was to peacefully persuade the Chokonen to leave their land and allow us to expand the town's mining opportunities. What you seem to have done is merely antagonise the Apaches and turn the only mining specialists for miles around against us.'

Fenraw glared at the mayor.

'Look Mr Fenraw, perhaps I am being a little harsh,' said Cleets. 'Please, sit down. Let us have a civil conversation. There is nothing that can't be sorted with some reasoned argument.'

Fenraw paused again then dropped himself into a leather chair at the side of the Mayor's desk. The mayor was forced to move his chair a little to face Fenraw.

'Now look Mr Fenraw...'

'You know that slaughter at the O'Brien's place had nothing to do with the Chokonen,' interrupted Fenraw.

'I know nothing of the sort, and if that is the case then I have to question your decision to attack the Apaches as even more misguided.'

'I only found out after the raid, but someone in this town must have known.'

The mayor kept his cool well. 'I can assure you that I, or any other members of the council, have no idea who committed that atrocity. Do you have your suspicions?'

'Yes I do,' muttered Fenraw. 'And when I get some proof there will be hell to pay.'

'Well might I suggest Mr Fenraw that you avail yourself with that proof at the earliest opportunity as without a doubt it would help to strengthen public opinion over your role as peacekeeper in this fine town.' The mayor's tone had an air of menace. 'I have to say that in the light of recent events your popularity amongst the residents of Wilburg appears to be very low.'

'If they believe that crap that Canton is spinning then they can go to hell,' spat Fenraw.

'Might I remind you that it is only the continued goodwill of those people that warrants the payments I make to you and your... group.'

'So what is your plan Mayor? What can I do to make the good people of Wilburg love me once again,' said Fenraw with a sarcastic sneer.

'Let me think now,' said the Mayor as he sat back in his chair deep in thought, as if he was formulating a national peace treaty.

Fenraw let out an audible sigh of exasperation.

'Mr Fenraw, I envisage two tasks that you must complete to restore your position as the keeper of the peace in Wilburg. Firstly, you should return to the O'Brien place and attempt to gather more information if, as you say, the attack there had nothing to do with the Chokonen. Secondly, on your way back here you should spend a little time with the McNairns and exert some level of diplomacy so that we may work closer with them in the future.'

'Go back to the mine?' yelled Fenraw. 'Those ingrates have as much affection for us as the Chokonen do.'

Cleets pushed back his chair and stood up sharply. Even on his feet he was not much taller than Fenraw was sitting down.

'You listen here Fenraw, that's my damn conditions. You are about as welcome in Wilburg as shit on a shoe at the moment,' he fumed. 'It won't do you, or your ragtag posse, any harm to step away for a little time and let things cool down. I don't give a good goddamn who killed those O'Briens but you make peace with the miners or don't come back into town.'

The Mayor pulled open a drawer, grabbed a small bundle of cash and threw it on the desk.

'Now take that money and do as I ask or that will be the last cent you see from me.'

Fenraw got up from his chair scowling but he said nothing. He stood defiantly in front of the Mayor, staring down at him, then he lifted the bundle of notes and left without a word.

VIII

It was early in the evening when Fenraw, Silent and the Kellys rode up to the McNairn's mine. The warm glow in the sky was in sharp contrast to the chilly reception they received. Lined up, and with weapons at the ready, was the traditional McNairn welcoming committee. Fenraw immediately scanned the unwelcome faces looking for Nancy and he spotted her standing squarely in the doorway of the house. At the centre of the group was Billy McNairn, shotgun in hand.

'What the hell are you doing here Fenraw,' he yelled. 'I ought to cut you down right now.'

'If you were going to do it, we would already be dead,' Fenraw called back. 'We're not here for a war Billy, not with you anyway. Cleets wants to help you protect his investment against any possible Indian trouble.'

'Trouble that you caused you damn fool,' spat Billy.

'What's done is done McNairn. We just want to help. Stay for a few days, that's all,' said Fred.

'We don't need that kind of help.'

'Look, McNairn we don't like this any more than you do,' shouted Fenraw. 'But if you want to ever buy even a bushel of corn or a pickaxe from Wilburg ever again you'd better show a little hospitality. That Cleets will cut off your supplies quicker than lightning so you can stay out here and eat rabbit for the rest of your days or ride on to the next town seventy five miles from here for your provisions.'

Billy McNairn's usually ruddy complexion turned a shade of purple.

'I'll tell you now,' he raged. 'I don't want any of you here but if you must stick around like a bad smell I want you out of my way. You can bunk down in the hut at the old mine entrance. The less I see of you Wilburg lackeys the better.'

'That suits us fine you bad tempered old pecker,' yelled Fenraw.

'Bobby! Get them out of my sight,' Billy shouted over to his younger brother.

'What?' said Bobby, a short, balding man who was still clutching a long-shafted hammer as a weapon. 'You can't expect me to...'

'… just get them out of my sight,' bellowed McNairn.

Bobby McNairn pushed open the door of the hut with the toe of his boot. Inside, under layers of dust, there was nothing but two wooden bunks, a table and a rusty old stove.

'Welcome to the McNairn family guest room,' he joked.

'Nice digs,' said Jim Kelly sarcastically.

'Who the hell has a table and no chairs,' said Fred, kicking up a cloud of dust as he walked round the room.

'I've got to say. If Billy had his way you would all be sleeping in a ditch miles from here,' said Bobby with a shrug. 'I'll get you a few chairs. Things will settle down. Just give my brother a bit of time to calm himself.'

George threw his blanket and canteen onto one of the bunks. 'That old goat won't ever calm down.'

'Hell it has got to be safer than waiting in that jailhouse like sitting ducks,' said Fenraw as he wiped the dust off the hut's only window and peered over to the McNairn's house.

'Things not going too well for you back in Wilburg either?' said Bobby.

'Let's just say we are happy to take our chances with you mudsills,' said Fred as he perched on the edge of the table.

'Hey, you really know how to make friends eh?' said Bobby with a smile. 'You keep talking like that and I'm liable to bring you a little lit stick of dynamite with your coffee.'

Fred smiled himself. 'Hell it's been so long since we met anyone who didn't want to put a bullet in us maybe we've forgotten how to.'

Fenraw threw Fred a dirty look intended to silence him.

'God damn Douglas, he might as well know, said Fred. 'You folks have got us down as Cleets strong arm and that ain't the case. I don't know why he hired us in the first place. He's done nothing but try to get us killed ever since.'

'That's enough Fred,' growled Fenraw.

Fred cursed under his breath and stormed outside. The atmosphere in the room was poisonous once again.

'Well maybe I had better leave you all to settle in,' said Bobby awkwardly. No one spoke and Silent stared at him intently.

'I'll get some supplies over later. I've got to go,' said Bobby as he walked out. As he closed the door behind him the room was still deadly quiet and Fenraw continued to peer out of the window.

Fred Kelly was standing a short distance away from the miner's hut smoking a small cheroot when Bobby walked past.

'You fellas don't seem too keen on your own company much my friend,' he said.

'Ah it's nothing,' said Fred as he let the smoke drift slowly from his mouth. 'He's just a pig-headed fool sometimes.'

'He don't seem too popular anywhere, far as I can see.'

'How do you mean?' asked Fred.

'The widow Nancy kicked him out on his ass real quick,' said Bobby.

Fred laughed. 'He ain't no Casanova that's for damn sure.'

'She even threw those gold bullets out behind him.'

'Gold bullets?' spluttered Fred.

'Gold slugs, yeh. Lead ain't good enough for them Apaches. That's what she pulled out of your friend,' said Bobby. 'I reckon she is sweet on him though.'

'Oh yeh,' Fred lit another cheroot and passed it to Bobby.

'Thanks friend,' the miner took a deep draw at the little cigar and exhaled the smoke slowly. 'Yeh, she ain't got nothing good to say about Fenraw but she still talks about him.'

'She's wasting her time. He's a heartless bastard,' said Fred.

'And he's a friend of yours?'

'Yeh,' Fred continued. 'We go way back. I can't spend no time with him that don't end in an argument but I would trust him with my life.'

'What about the tall guy with the light hair? He don't say much,' said Bobby.

'He's got no tongue. Don't ask me why. He can make some sounds but he chooses not to. Cold-blooded killer as well, he don't seem care what happens to himself.'

'And the other two?'

'They are my brothers,' said Fred.

'You mean your...' Bobby stuttered.

'I mean my brothers fool. My god-damn brothers,' Fred spat. 'Why? Do you think we are all "brothers".'

'I didn't mean to...' Bobby looked embarrassed and stared down at the dust.

Fred realised he had reacted too harshly and he patted Bobby on the shoulder.

'I'm sorry man. Like I said, we just ain't used to seeing a friendly face.'

Fred and Bobby smoked in silence for a little while and watched the last rays of daylight disappear over the horizon. The mine was still now but a few people with oil lamps could be spotted milling around near the McNairn house.

Fred took a long look right across the mine and all its outbuildings. 'Things don't seem too bad out here.'

'It ain't easy but its home... for now. I just hope this beef with the Chokonen fades real soon, especially as it was all a waste of time.'

Fred turned to look at Bobby directly. 'What do you mean, waste of time?'

'That attack at the O'Brien place wasn't no Apache attack,' explained Bobby. 'Just after it happened we heard some horses head past here towards Wilburg.'

Fred spun round and grabbed Bobby firmly by the throat.

'You had better be telling me the truth fella. I've heard enough lies around these parts.'

Bobby was shocked but he broke free from Fred's grip. He took a step back but kept the cheroot clenched between his teeth.

'Fenraw knows you damn fool,' he shouted. 'Billy told me. The Chokonen had no reason to attack the O'Briens. Jesus, they got gold bullets. What the hell are they going to get? Those homesteaders lived a poor but righteous existence, they didn't have nothing to steal.'

Fred felt his anger with Billy subside only to be replaced with fresh fury at Fenraw. He snorted loudly but said nothing.

Bobby dropped the end of his cheroot in the dust. 'I'd better go.'

Fred placed his hand on Bobby's shoulder to placate him.

'Look, I'm sorry. I lost my temper. There ain't much truth around Wilburg, I've forgotten what it sounds like.'

'Okay, okay,' said Bobby as he moved away and smiled slightly. 'Jesus, you fellas are highly strung.'

'You take it easy brother,' said Fred.

'Are you going back in?'

'I'll just let that old goat stew a while. Maybe take a little ride around the country out here.'

Bobby screwed up his face a little. 'Are you sure? There is a lot of unfriendliness out there in the dark.'

'I've spent my life in the shadows,' Fred laughed. 'It don't bother me none. I'll see you later.'

As Bobby walked back to the farmhouse he heard Fred speak quietly to his horse as he got in the saddle then ride out into the night.

When Fred Kelly eventually returned to the old miner's hut Fenraw seemed pleased to see him.

'Hey, take a seat. The miners brought over some more furniture. Seems we are not as unpopular as plague dogs after all.'

Fred stayed on his feet. 'I ought to break one of them chairs over your damn head. Why didn't you tell us who actually attacked the O'Briens? And what about those gold bullets?'

'If you want gold bullets just ride back to the Chokonen camp and you'll get plenty... right in the chest,' said Fenraw angrily.

'What about the O'Briens?' shouted Fred.

'I don't know who killed them. That's why I never said anything. I just don't think it was the Apaches.'

'Jesus,' said Fred. 'And you led us right in to that massacre?'

'I only found out from Nancy. That fool Billy McNairn saw some people heading back to Wilburg on the night of the attack. He just never told us.'

'Man that's a sweet bit of pillow talk,' growled Fred. 'You and the widow sharing little secrets while my brother is getting his arm stitched together and the whole town ready to have us swinging on a rope.'

'Oh that's a crock. Sit your ass down and quit whining,' Fenraw sneered.

'No, dammit. You better tell me what you know or this thing ends right here.'

'What?' said Fenraw. 'What? Seems like you and your little friend out there have all the answers. The Chokonen didn't attack the O'Briens and I don't know who did. Cleets and his cronies are crooks, Canton's men are bandits and the people of Wilburg are assholes. That's it. The whole thing has turned to shit, that's all you need to know.'

'So why the hell are you still here? What is there to stop you riding out right now and leave us and all this trouble behind,' said Fred angrily.

'Because I ain't got nowhere else to go,' yelled Fenraw as he banged his fists onto the table.

Suddenly Fred knew that he had pushed too far. He remembered the time he had trekked for four days to visited Fenraw at his cabin outside of Breck-inridge. He had intended to lure Fenraw away to a real dirty job tracking down two killers but when he saw how happy he was at home with Jessie and little Jimmy he had lied and claimed he was just passing through. Fenraw looked different now, his eyes were permanently cold and angry and his furrowed brow had dug deep lines across his forehead. Fred slumped into a chair at the other side of the table and they both sat in silence.

Despite their sparse accommodation, Fenraw's posse had settled overnight in the miners cabin quite well. Bobby enlisted some of the other men and they brought over a little food and some wood for the rusted stove at the back of the room. As the first beams of morning light filtered through the dirty window Fenraw woke up with the same jolt that he always did. The miners had already started working and, although they were some distance away, they could still be heard from the hut. Fenraw got up from the bed quietly as the Kelly brothers were still asleep. Silent looked as if he was asleep but his body seemed stiff and alert. Fenraw wondered if he was ever truly at rest.

After sipping on a cup of cold coffee Fenraw took a walk outside, closing the hut door behind him gently. It was a cool morning with a little mist way in the distance. It was good to look out into open space once again instead of looking at Wilburg's dusty main street and its mean-spirited people. Soon he spotted something that made his spirits rise a little more. Nancy McNairn was approaching on her horse. Her dark hair was pulled back tightly and secured with a black velvet band, her red lips looked full and fresh even this early in the morning and the rifle across her lap glistened in the low sunlight.

Fenraw stepped forward into her path and she brought her horse to a halt.

'Why good morning widow McNairn,' shouted Fenraw. 'Come to check on your guests?'

'Go to hell Fenraw, I ride this way every morning to exercise my horse. Don't flatter yourself and get out of my way.'

Fenraw stood defiantly still but Nancy made no effort to ride around him.

'What happened to the hospitality I received here last time,' he said.

'We McNairns wouldn't let a dog die out here and you were no different.'

Fenraw stared at Nancy directly. 'So why are you giving us board now?'

'Because you damn near blackmailed us, that's why,' said Nancy with a sneer.

'Look, we just want to sit it out here for a while just in case the Chokonen do get riled,' reasoned Fenraw.

'They've already been here you fool,' snorted Nancy. 'We buried three good men a few days ago.'

'What happened?'

'The night after you left some Apaches attacked. They set fire to a few small outbuildings and fired some shots into the house. We fought back but three of our men were hit badly.'

'Why the hell didn't you send word to us at Wilburg?' said Fenraw angrily.

'Because you caused the damn problem in the first place,' yelled Nancy, her face red with anger. 'It wasn't a full attack anyway, just some young braves making a stand.'

Fenraw stared at the ground like a scolded schoolboy. 'Well we are here now. If they come back we'll be ready.'

'They ain't going to come back, Billy put things right.'

'What the hell did he do?' said Fenraw. 'Run to their camp with a wagon of trinkets and whiskey? Those people only care about vengeance.'

'There's other ways to deal with people than shooting them you heathen.'

'What did he say to them,' asked Fenraw.

'Ask him your damn self, you know where he is.'

'I would if I could get near the old fool without him squealing like a stuck pig.'

Nancy smiled a little but tried to cover it up. 'He hates you Fenraw but he is a reasonable man. Maybe in the circles you mix in that's a rare trait.'

A shiver ran across Fenraw's back but he was not sure if it came from the chilly morning air or his proximity to Nancy.

'Okay, I'll see him now,' said Fenraw with a sigh of resignation. 'Why don't you let me a hitch a ride with you?'

Nancy laughed sarcastically and as she turned and rode off she shouted back, 'Make your own way there mercenary.'

As the dust she kicked up settled around Fenraw he watched her go. She spurred her horse on and her ponytail swayed in the wind. She was a fine figure of a women even in those old working duds. Fenraw felt a warm glow deep in the pit of his stomach that even his usual bitterness couldn't extinguish.

After a scant breakfast with his friends Fenraw made some vague excuse and made his way over to the McNairn house. As he tapped on the door and waited he felt a little tingle of anticipation as he prepared to see Nancy again. There was no answer and when his patience imploded after only a short while he banged the door impatiently. One of the miners appeared from the side of the house carrying an axe. Fenraw immediately reached for his pistol and the miner froze to the spot.

'Hey, take it easy,' said the miner.

'I've come to see Billy,' barked Fenraw.

'He's over at the creek, just behind that small hill over there.'

'Where's the widow?'

'Oh she ain't here. She's gone into town,' the miner said slyly.

'What the hell are you smirking at?' said Fenraw.

'Nothing my friend. Nothing at all.'

Fenraw felt as if he was the butt of some kind of joke amongst the miners. The lovesick fool? Anything like that could only undermine his position. Any warm feelings he had were swamped with the familiar rush of anger and bitterness. He said nothing to the miner and stormed off towards the creek.

Billy McNairn was sitting quietly at the edge of the creek with his fishing rod dipped in the still, clear water and his shotgun on the ground at arms distance. He heard Fenraw coming and spun round with the weapon cocked and ready.

'Fenraw. What the hell are you doing here?' Billy's tone was unwelcome but he laid his shotgun back on the ground and continued to focus on the spot where his fishing line met the surface of the water.

'I understand you spoke to the Chokonen,' said Fenraw.

Billy sighed a little. 'Fenraw, you really know how to take the best out of a good day.'

Fenraw said nothing but stood behind Billy defiantly.

'Well sit the hell down,' said Billy. 'You're scaring the damn fish.'

Fenraw moved reluctantly but chose a rock some distance away.

'Not there,' barked Billy. 'Your shadow is on the water. Sit there.' He pointed to a rock on his right. It was closer to Billy than Fenraw would have liked but he sat down anyway. Both men sat in silence and stared at the water.

'What the hell is going on between you and those Chokonen anyway?' asked Fenraw eventually.

'Look Fenraw,' said Billy wearily. 'I've spoke to Bobby and maybe you ain't the devils we first thought but I will always do what is right for my family and my miners. I don't give a red cent for your posse or those assholes back in Wilburg so let's just get that straight.'

'Okay, okay, I get it. But dealing with the Apaches?'

'They are just family folks like the rest of us,' said Billy. 'Well most of us anyway. Apart from the ones that only care about money or violence.'

'What are you getting at?' asked Fenraw angrily.

'Hey, if the shoe fits wear it.'

Both men scowled at each other then almost simultaneously their frowns faded.

'Maybe you're right,' said Fenraw quietly.

'If you had a family son, maybe you would truly understand.'

Fenraw felt his chest and throat tighten a little and he avoided Billy's eyes.

'Do you have one?' said Billy.

Fenraw kept his gaze fixed on the distance. 'Back in Breckinridge once. But there is nothing to go back to now.' Fenraw cursed under his breath, furious that he had given even a little of his history away.

Billy sensed that he had touched a nerve and kept a respectful silence for a little while.

'I've seen too many of my people die just to get here Fenraw,' he continued. 'I sure as hell don't want to lose any more. We can make a living here with the copper we mine. Sure the gold on the Chokonen land would make our lives a lot easier but it ain't worth dying for.'

'It's a pity Cleets don't feel that way,' said Fenraw.

'Cleets only wants it because it's there and he don't need to put his skinny ass in danger to get it,' ranted Billy.

The miner threw his rod to the ground and reached for a small bottle of whisky in the leather bag that lay in front of him.

'Dammit Fenraw, how in the hell did you get involved with those snakes in the first place?' said Billy. 'You sure don't look like no fool.'

Fenraw picked up a small stone and threw it as far as he could into the creek before he spoke. 'Just looking for a dollar, same as everybody else. Didn't expect to get dragged into all this. I figured it was just another job keeping the peace amongst the drunks and rowdies.'

'So why did Cleets call you? Seems that that's a job any upstanding fella could do?'

Fenraw took some time to give Billy a reply, as if he was looking for the answer himself.

'Maybe I've got a reputation for getting the job done... regardless.'

Billy passed the bottle of Scotch to Fenraw. 'Son, maybe you really don't care who gets hurt.'

'Maybe not,' said Fenraw as he slugged down the whiskey.

After a little while and some more conversation Fenraw left the creek and walked the long way back to his meagre accommodation. While he and Billy could certainly not be described as good friends, Fenraw mentally pushed the Scot back a few places in the list of people he hated. As he approached the front porch of the miner's hut Fred Kelly appeared and shut the door behind him.

'Let me in, I need a drink,' said Fenraw as he tried to push past Fred.

Kelly gave Fenraw a push to the chest that was firm enough to force him back a few steps.

'Where the hell have you been?'

'Down at the creek with McNairn,' said Fenraw.

'You didn't kill the old fool and leave him there did you?'

'What are you talking about? Of course not.' Fenraw's voice was full of indignation.

'Good,' said Fred. 'Because we got company.' He pushed open the cabin door with a flourish and as Fenraw walked inside he noticed Nancy sitting at the table sipping some coffee with Jim and George. Silent sat in the corner cleaning his weapons.

'Nancy,' Fenraw let her name slip too easily from his lips and quickly adopted a sarcastic tone. 'To what do we owe the pleasure?'

'Nancy is just back from town,' said Jim. 'She's got something to tell us.'

'Oh yeh,' said Fenraw cautiously.

'Yeh,' said Nancy. 'But the chilly reception I'm getting from you Douglas ain't nothing compared to what I got in Wilburg.'

'Seems someone in town is setting the McNairns up as some kind of Indian lovers,' said George.

'I may not be high society but some of them townsfolk were downright hostile,' said Nancy.

Fred Kelly sat down at the table with the rest.

'Something is going on Fenraw,' he said. 'If they are spreading poison about the McNairns then they are sure as hell dragging our names through the dirt as well.'

Fenraw continued to stand at the door. 'Don't be an old maid Kelly. We are still the law in Wilburg whatever the local mudsills say.'

'That Canton seems to strolling around like the Pope of cowtown though,' said Nancy. 'Him and his dirty sidekicks.'

Fenraw sensed a real vengeance in her words.

'What happened? Did they touch you?'

'It was nothing I can't handle,' she replied.

Fenraw spun round and reached for the door handle. 'Why those dirty...'

'Sit on your ass Fenraw,' yelled Nancy. 'I can take care of myself.'

Her yell stopped Fenraw in his tracks. He looked at her sitting at the table with her eyes burning brightly and her cheeks tinged with red.

'Why you ain't much of a lady are you?' he said.

'No, but she's all woman,' quipped Jim and he reached forward to slap his brother George on the back.

The Kelly's whooped with laughter as Fenraw walked over to the table and sat down himself. He kept his eyes on Nancy and she stared back, each waiting for the other to back down. Fenraw was the first to blink and he smiled and shook his head as he looked down. Nancy sat back in the chair with a look of satisfaction.

'One of the miners told me you went to see my brother-in law,' she said. 'Did you sort things out?'

'With that old goat?' Fenraw sneered.

'He's a good man Douglas. He cares about his family and that includes everyone at this mine.'

'Including us?' growled Fenraw.

'Yes, while you are all our guests he would fight to help you all, even if you don't deserve it.'

Fenraw leaned forward in his chair. 'If this hut fell down a mine shaft right now he wouldn't give a damn.'

'Well I certainly wouldn't,' screamed Nancy as she pushed back her chair violently and made for the door. 'Douglas Fenraw you are an insufferable, mean-spirited ass. God help the rest of you.' She slammed the door behind her with such force that a layer of dust shook down from the roof.

Fenraw looked around the table, everyone was staring at him. Even Silent peered over from the corner.

'What?' shouted Fenraw.

'Don't be a fool Douglas. Go after her,' said Fred quietly.

'Why?'

'Fenraw, I ain't been around a woman for some time but even I can see that she is crazy about you,' said Jim.

Fenraw remained in his seat defiantly.

'Hell you better go after her or I might have to,' added George with a sly smile. 'You know what they say, a woman scorned might just grab a hold of the next man she sees and I ain't going to let that fine piece go spare.'

Fenraw stood up and noticed them all smiling. 'Okay, I'll go after her but only to protect her from your evil clutches.' As he pointed at George a tiny smiled tried to crack through his grim expression.

'Yeh, yeh,' said George. 'Whatever you say.'

'Hey Fenraw,' Jim yelled over as Fenraw reached for the door.

'What?'

'Ask her if she has a sister.'

The Kellys roared with laughter as Fenraw left the room.

Nancy was more than half way back to the McNairn house when Fenraw spotted her. She had a determined stride and Fenraw had to run to catch up with her. He checked himself mentally for running after a woman but the feeling inside him was stronger and it spurred him on.

'Nancy, hold up,' he shouted.

She turned and saw him approaching but kept on walking.

'God dammit woman I ain't gonna chase you.' Fenraw stopped and bent over a little to regain his breath and composure.

Nancy stopped walking but stood her ground. 'Come here then.'

'Listen McNairn, I've followed you further than any woman I've known and I ain't taking a step more.'

'Well where does that leave us,' said Nancy with a smile.

'About fifty foot apart,' yelled Fenraw.

'So how do you intend to resolve that you stubborn old mule.'

'I'm damned if I know.'

They stood in the bright sunlight staring at each other with neither of them willing to give up any ground.

'Maybe if we each took a step forward at a time we could resolve this,' shouted Nancy.

'You go first then,' said Fenraw.

'No Douglas. Together.'

Nancy started to move and Fenraw followed her. Each took a step grudgingly, watching the other to make sure they kept up their part of the deal. Eventually their steps grew more rapid. When they met in the middle there was a moment's stillness then they fell into a tight embrace with their lips locked together. Fenraw's senses were inflamed. A woman. A full-bodied, warm, soft and sweet smelling woman was in his arms once again. He remembered this feeling but this time it was different. For as long as he could remember he had kept his emotions locked away tightly within himself for self-preservation but now he could hold them back no longer. A wave of passion and lust swept over him as they gripped each other tightly. Fenraw felt a violent stab of regret deep in his chest and then it was gone.

Jim Canton strode down Wilburg's main street like an emperor. Almost all the able men in town were now under his command. Sure it was Cleets' money but it was he who decided how it should be spent. Maybe his force were not the best specimens of fighting manhood either but that would change. As word spread that he was willing to make rich men out of able hellraisers he could replace the weak links in his chain. Godammit, if he could raise the money himself he could tell Cleets to go to hell. Fortune favours the strong... and ruthless.

Lost in his own thoughts, Canton wandered close to the jailhouse. A tall, distinguished looking gent was banging the door of the building with his fist. The man was smartly dressed and well-groomed but even with his suit on it was obvious he had a muscular build. Canton noticed a few of his latest employees loafing nearby and he gestured sharply for them to join him. Three yokels, all armed, shuffled into place behind Canton.

'Good morning my friend,' Canton shouted to the man. 'Can I help you?'

'You can if you know where Douglas Fenraw is.'

'Ah, a friend of Mr Fenraw. Please let me introduce myself. James Canton at your service.' Canton thrust his hand forward.

'Canton eh?'

'James Canton, that is correct sir. And you are?'

The stranger looked at Canton's hand, then grudgingly shook it.

'Jack Harris.'

'Harris,' said Canton. 'No relation to our esteemed lawman then?'

Harris was suspicious and stared at Canton. 'No but we've been in a few scrapes together and no mistake.'

'Well I'm afraid Mr Fenraw is away on town business Mr Harris and it is uncertain when he will return. If you so wish I could have one of my men get some feed and fresh water for your horse so that you may be on your way.'

'No,' said Harris. 'I'll wait.'

'I can assure you Mr Harris that you will have a long wait,' said Canton insistently.

'Look fancy pants, I'll wait so you just move along.'

Canton could hear the men behind him giggling and it made Harris' attitude even harder to take.

'I warn you Mr Harris, in Mr Fenraw's absence I am responsible for keeping good order in this town.'

'Beat it,' shouted Harris. 'I know who you are. Jim Canton. Wanted for criminal damage in Flagstaff, assault in Prescott, horse theft in Winslow and a whole load of other damn things. Why I could pull a bounty on you right now but I'm too damn tired.'

A furious rage built up inside Canton. 'That is a damn lie Sir. I'll have you before the judge for that libel.' Canton roared at the men behind him, 'Get him.'

The three locals moved towards Harris unsteadily, each looking to the others for confirmation that they were doing the right thing. The hesitation was all Harris needed and he despatched the first man with a clear shot to the head. The other two fired wildly and while Harris focused his attention on them Canton moved a few steps to the side and took aim. His bullet was far more accurate than his new recruits and it plunged into Harris' shoulder and sent him crashing onto the window of the jailhouse. Harris did not fall through the window but some shards of glass lodged in his back and the slicing pain made him drop his gun on the porch. Canton relished the sight of an unarmed man in front and took the opportunity to fire two more shots into his legs. As Harris crashed to the ground both of Canton's foot soldiers ran over and started to deliver heavy kicks to his body and head.

Canton let the beating continue and watched with relish before he finally called the massacre to an end. All three of them watched Harris try to get to his feet but he could barely lift his head off the ground.

'Shot down in the street by a felon and some retards,' he croaked. 'Ain't there no damn law in this hellhole?'

'I am the law,' said Canton as he delivered the bullet that sent Harris to meet his maker.

When Fenraw returned to the miner's hut over a day later the Kelly's were not only bored but inquisitive. No matter how much they questioned him, Fenraw gave nothing away other than orders to pack up and head for Wilburg. The time he had spent with Nancy had left him with a warm feeling that he struggled to suppress. The Kelly brothers and Silent noticed the change in his disposition but only smirked to themselves. Hell, even his last meeting with Billy

McNairn had been less than antagonistic. As they all rode back towards Wilburg, Fenraw felt oddly positive. Good feelings like this were alien to him but after his time with Nancy, the McNairns grudgingly on their side and the possibility of avoiding an all out Apache war he felt that maybe in Wilburg things might work out if the perpetrators of the O'Brien massacre could be brought to justice. All those thoughts crumbled in the dust as soon as he saw the welcoming committee outside town.

A few miles back Fenraw had noticed a little kicked-up dust cloud in the distance but he knew that some folk did a little rabbit hunting in the surrounding countryside so he thought no more about it. It had obviously been a scout given the job of announcing their return. Already waiting for them outside of town were around thirty men, fully armed and spread out should Fenraw and his partners try to escape. Fenraw had no intentions of avoiding this motley posse and he rode straight towards the centre of the group.

'This don't look good,' said Jim Kelly.

'Just keep riding,' said Fenraw. 'Don't give them any reason to shoot. We'll sort this out later.'

Fenraw looked over to Silent who was starting to weigh up his options. 'Silent', shouted Fenraw but the mute just stared ahead. 'Silent. Don't do anything stupid.' They finally made eye contact and Silent nodded slowly.

The mob was made up of Wilburg citizens and a few drifters who just happened to be in town. Many of them looked ill at ease with their weapons but slightly bolstered by the size of their posse. Fenraw wondered how many of them would really have the stomach for a fight. Canton, Averill and Dodge were at the centre of the group. They beamed as Fenraw's group approached, as if they were a trio of Generals marshalling a crack army unit instead of a ragtag mob of mercenaries.

'Why Douglas how are you?' crowed Canton as Fenraw and his friends pulled up their horses in front of him.

'I was fine until I saw you,' growled Fenraw.

'Now, now Douglas. There is no need for that foul attitude. We are merely here to escort you back into town,' said Canton.

'We know the way,' replied Fenraw.

'Yeh, ' shouted Fred with a mocking tone. 'No need for the escort. A little town parade would have been good enough to welcome us home.'

'The only parade you will see is a funeral parade you black dog,' shouted Dodge.

'Now, now Mr Dodge there is no need for that yet,' said Canton as he raised his hands in a gesture intended to calm the confrontation. 'I must say though Douglas that you are required to accompany us into town until certain accusations have been laid to rest.'

'What accusations?' shouted George.

'It has come to our attention that you and your friends may have had more than a little to do with the attack on the O'Brien place. The subsequent attack on the Chokonen may now have contributed to real danger now facing the good people of Wilburg.' Canton relished his little speech and puffed his chest out with pride.

'That's a crock Canton and you know it,' said Fenraw.

Averill took his turn to showboat to the audience. 'Either way Fenraw, you and your friends throw down your weapons and get off your horses, we are taking you to jail.'

'Go to hell,' hissed Fenraw.

The Wilburg posse tensed and pointed their weapons at Fenraw.

'Come now Douglas,' said Canton. 'Unless you want us to finish things off right here.'

Fenraw knew that Canton would gladly do that given half a chance so he turned to his friends. 'Okay, let's do what this jackass wants.'

Silent was first off his horse and he stepped over towards Averill and placed his pistol on the ground.

'See,' said Averill triumphantly. 'Your little dummy friend has the right idea.'

Almost before he had finished his sentence, Silent leaped forward, grabbed Averill's leg and brought him crashing down off his horse. Before Averill got the chance to draw breath Silent had a knife to his throat.

Thirty fingers hovered over their triggers, unsure what to do.

Averill tried to shout but the knife was pressed down on his windpipe and a small line of blood was visible on the weapon's sharp edge.

'This ain't going to work Fenraw,' said a surprisingly distressed Canton. 'Tell your boy to stand down.'

Fenraw paused for a moment, almost willing Silent to cut that snake's throat, but he knew it would mean death for all of them.

'No Silent,' he shouted eventually. 'Not now.'

Silent looked at Fenraw for what seemed like an age then he dropped the knife and let Averill fall to the ground gasping. Dodge swung his rifle butt at the back of Silent's head sending him crashing into the dirt.

Canton regained his composure quickly and he barked his orders at his flunkies. 'Tie them up and get their horses and guns. These traitors can walk back to Wilburg.'

'What about him?' said one of the posse, pointing at Silent's prone body.

'Give him a kick,' shouted Averill as he climbed back onto his horse unsteadily. 'And if he don't wake then drag him back to town.'

A familiar dark cloud of hate and anger settled over Fenraw once again as he and the Kellys had their hands roughly tied by some of the cackling mob. The warmth and optimism that Nancy had given him was now just a distant memory.

Cleets made his grand entrance into the jailhouse with Canton and Averill at either side. It was midday. Just the right time for a fine performance in front of all the good townsfolk of Wilburg. More of Canton's new recruits followed them until the building was almost full. Fenraw knew what was coming. Let the show begin.

'I have to say Mr Fenraw, this is not the scenario I had in mind when I invited you to keep the peace in this fine town,' said Cleets as he walked as close to Fenraw's cell as he felt comfortable.

'You can talk all you want in front of these local dimwits Cleets but you know that throwing me behind bars is a pile of bullshit.' Fenraw lay back on his bunk. 'Go on. What's the charge? Tell them all what you'd like them to think.'

Cleets went a little red with anger but held back his temper. 'Why you are uncouth Mr Fenraw. I hired you to protect those miners not start an Indian war that puts our whole town at risk.'

Fred Kelly stood in the next cell and pointed his finger at Canton. 'Hell Mayor, if you want to know who started all this then just look at the man on your right. It was his thugs that killed the O'Briens and he sure as hell knew it would lead to this.'

Cleets kept his eye on Fenraw and refused to even look at Fred. 'I will not converse with that... man.'

'Why you...' Fred kicked the cell door with such a fury that some of the men in the room reached for their guns. 'I knew it from the start. Nothing changes. You Wilburg folks can all go to hell.'

'Come on brother,' said George as he pulled Fred back from the door to the rear of the cell. 'No amount of sense is going to reach these crackers.'

Fenraw still lay on the bed but he was trying to hold back his anger.

'Look Cleets, you set us up from the very beginning. So make your speech to your adoring audience and get the hell out. Come back when you've got a mind to set us free.'

'God damn you Fenraw,' yelled the Mayor. 'The only time you'll get out of here is when you take a walk to the hangman's noose. You and your bandit friends here are trying to stir up a whirlwind of trouble in this town and I don't know why. And now you've got them damn immigrant miners on your side hell knows what you are planning.'

'Maybe Mr Fenraw is looking to start a new dynasty out there with the merry widow,' said Canton with a smirk. 'Maybe they are all planning to freeze everyone in Wilburg out of their share of the gold.'

'What damn share,' yelled Fenraw. 'That gold is heading straight for the pockets of Cleets and his cronies.'

'Mr Fenraw,' roared the mayor in a voice so loud that it stunned almost everyone in the room. 'Every cent that that gold makes will benefit this town and its people. That's something that a mercenary like you must find hard to understand.'

Fenraw stood up leisurely and walked to the front of the cell slowly, clapping his hands in sarcastic applause as he went.

'Bravo Mayor, Bravo. You've really gave these good people here something to think about.' Fenraw looked around the room in disgust. Everyone of them were there no doubt because Canton had jammed a few dollars in their pockets. He looked at Canton and Averill and their smug grins made him want to reach through the bars and throttle them. Then he looked at the Mayor, so red-faced with anger that he actually looked as if he believed his own lies. Fenraw stared directly at him.

'You can go to hell Cleets. You know the truth. You don't care who dies as long as your pockets are filled with gold.'

Cleets took a deep breath and regained his composure a little.

'Mr Fenraw,' he hissed. 'You and your friends will receive a fair trial and, if you are found to be guilty, you will all be publicly hanged.'

'Fair trial my ass,' growled Fenraw.

'Go to hell Cleets,' yelled Fred and he hurled a tin cup that had been left in the cell at the Mayor's head.

The cup glanced off Cleets' head and he was more startled than hurt by the flying missile.

'Savages. Savages,' he shouted and began pushing through the crowd to leave. 'Mr Averill, you stay with these heathens. No food, no water until I say and if they try anything unseemly then shoot them dead.'

'With pleasure,' said Averill slumping down into an old leather chair at Fenraw's desk.

The crowd filed out and Canton was the last to leave. 'You take good care of our friends here Clancy.'

'You got no problem there Jim,' said Averill as he cradled his shotgun on his lap. 'We are all going to get along just fine.'

As evening settled in the jailhouse Clancy Averill was quite enjoying his new role as key-holder and he was holding court with his captive audience.

'This is quite a turnaround Mr Fenraw,' he crowed as he strutted around the jailhouse with his thumbs lodged behind the lapels of his jacket. 'Less than a week ago you were leading us all into certain death as our proud leader, yet here you are now, caged like a common horse thief.'

Fenraw refused to acknowledge him and lay on his bunk with his hat covering his eyes.

'All along you and your motley bandits were plotting to drag the good people of this town through the very gates of hell,' Averill continued.

'Shut your mouth Averill,' shouted Fred. 'You know this is a damn set up.'

'I know nothing of the sort my dark friend,' said Averill. 'Your appetite for conspiracy is commendable but I can assure you that my only desire is to protect the good people of Wilburg. Something you and your amigos may find hard to digest.'

'You don't give a damn about those folks,' said George as he moved towards the front of his cell. 'You just want a share of that gold same as Cleets and all his jackals.'

Averill walked over to the coffee pot that was brewing by the fire.

'My, my, you Kelly boys have a very base understanding of town politics. The Mayor may see it fit to reward myself and Mr Canton but we only have the best interests of the town at heart,' he said smugly as he poured himself a hot brew.

'Bullshit', hissed George.

Averill strolled over to Silent's cell and tapped his cup gently on the bars. 'What about you my deadly friend. Nothing to say?'

Averill laughed at his own wit but his smile faded as Silent leapt to his feet and moved to the front of his cell. Before Silent could get near, Averill threw the contents of his cup in Silent's face. The coffee stung his skin and he dropped to his knees and let out a guttural gasp.

Averill was shocked by his own brutality but pleased to see Silent's pain. 'Murdering scum,' he yelled.

As he stepped back from Silent's cell he passed just close enough to George

Kelly who reached through the bars and grabbed Averill by the neck, pulling his head against the cell door with a crack. Before Averill could gather his senses, Fred Kelly handed George a small knife. George ran the blade down Averill's cheek opening the flesh wide then held the tip of the weapon to the side of his throat.

'Give me those damn keys or I'll cut you open you dandy son of a bitch,' shouted George.

'You think we didn't keep a little something in these cells for times like these,' said Fred. 'Now make with those keys or my brother will cut your throat and we'll drag you in here in pieces.'

Averill was in pieces already, his head throbbed, his cheek was burning with pain and he could feel the George's knife digging into his neck even deeper. He fumbled wildly for the keys, anything to get him some relief. As he passed them to Fred, George banged Averill's head against the bars once more then pushed him to the ground. With their jailer crumpled on the floor, Fred set himself and his brothers free then moved to Fenraw's cell.

'Don't bother with me damn you,' yelled Fenraw. 'Get Silent out.'

Fred opened the door to Silent's cell and helped him to his feet. He was conscious but his face was red and sticky.

'Get some towels and cold water,' Fred called over to George as he helped Silent over to a chair. He threw the keys to Jim. 'Let Fenraw out. And watch that damned Averill.'

Averill was groaning quietly but moving very little. As soon as Fenraw was freed he ran over to his desk drawer and pulled out a small, leather pouch.

He moved over to Silent's chair and placed a comforting hand on his shoulder. 'Just sit back friend. I've got something here that's going to sting like hell but do you a lot of good.'

Fenraw began dabbing some lotion on Silent's skin. He had bought the small bottle from a snake oil salesman back in Breckinridge. He did not know what the hell it was but he had used it on some of his many cuts and bruises and he knew it worked. He also knew that it must hurt like hell but Silent barely flinched, he just stared into the distance. Fenraw wondered just what exactly was Silent's story? He almost seemed to relish the pain as if he was punishing himself for some past indiscretion. Silent knew Fenraw was looking at him but as soon as the lotion had been applied he dropped his gaze to the floor.

Fred had moved over to the window and was peering out cautiously.

'Free at last Douglas ,' he said. 'But what the hell do we do next?'

When Clancy Averill came to he was no longer the lord of the jailhouse but strapped to a chair in the cell where Silent had been. The door was wide open but Silent stood guard staring at him. His skin had been treated but his eyes were still burning with anger. Jim Kelly was keeping watch at the window and Fred, George and Fenraw sat at a desk talking quietly.

'All we have is Averill's shotgun and his pistol with only four bullets,' said Fred.

'Don't forget the knife,' added George.

'Yeh brother,' said Fred sarcastically. 'Let's take on the town with that damn potato peeler.'

'Dammit Fred, if push comes to shove...'

'Forget the knife,' said Fenraw. 'We've got to get out there and get some weapons and horses and we've got to do it before dawn.'

'Out there?' said Fred incredulously. 'The whole town wants us to hang.'

'What's the alternative,' growled Fenraw. 'Sit here and wait for them all to come back. We've got to get armed and get the hell out of here. If we can make it back to the mine we might have a chance.'

'The mine? They almost want us to hang as much as the folks of Wilburg do,' said Fred.

'Almost,' said Fenraw. 'And that's a whole lot better than the chance we are going to get here.'

'Our chances are getting slimmer,' said Jim with a loud whisper. 'Someone's coming to check up on Averill.'

George leapt to his feet and reached for Averill's shotgun.

'Not the damn gun,' said Fenraw urgently. 'Want to wake up the whole town? Use the poker.'

George moved to the fireplace, picked up an iron poker and took his place at the side of the door. The door swung open but before their visitor could register surprise at the sight of Fred and Fenraw sitting at the desk he was knocked unconscious. George dragged his body into the room and closed the door quietly.

'Looks like we've got another gun.'

As George turned the body over to search for weapons and ammo Fenraw noticed that the unlucky visitor was no more than a teenage boy. He felt a wave of revulsion as he thought how Cleets and his cronies did not give a damn who got hurt in their pursuit of riches. Fenraw stormed over to the fireplace and grabbed a jug of fresh water from the shelf above it. Pushing Silent aside he strode into the cell and threw the contents of the jug in Averill's face.

'I'm awake god dammit, I'm awake,' gasped Averill.

Fenraw grabbed him roughly by the throat. 'I ain't got time to argue with you Averill so you tell me right now who hit the O'Brien's place or I will leave you alone with Silent here and find out what I want someplace else.'

'Douglas, you have to be reasonable,' spluttered Averill.

'Right now dammit,' said Fenraw as he tightened his grip on Averill's windpipe.

Averill was in no position to bargain, he could see the hate in Silent's eyes and the willingness to do him great damage.

'It was Cleets' idea,' he said weakly. 'He sent out Canton, Dodge, myself and some hired hands to carry out that hellish task. I was against it from the very start but Cleets insisted it was for the greater good. I wanted no part of the butchery. You've got to believe me.'

Fenraw let go his grip and stepped back.

'You've had the truth Fenraw. Now set me free,' pleaded Averill. 'Please now. Let's be civil.'

Fenraw turned and walked out of the cell.

'He's all yours but keep him quiet,' said Fenraw as he walked past silent.

Before Averill could scream Silent was upon him.

Mayor Cleets was not a man who believed in living frugally and his own home was equally as opulent as the council chambers. In his study he sat in a carefully upholstered leather chair which almost engulfed his small frame. Gilded gas lamps let off a warm glow and expensive cigar smoke wafted around the room. Cleets was sharing a fine bottle of Whisky with Jed Ryker and Nate Rogers.

'This is a fine Scotch Mayor,' said Rogers as he swirled the amber liquid round his glass. 'Pity the other Scottish import we have round these parts is proving to be such a pain in the ass.'

'Those damn miners are going to start a revolution if they get in tow with Fenraw and his boys again,' added Ryker.

'Gentlemen,' said Cleets quietly. 'Mr Fenraw and his boys won't make it past the rope. Of that I can assure you.'

'Why the hell did you hire him in the first place Jacob?' said Ryker.

'Mr Fenraw has served his purpose Jed. I brought him in to find out just how bad our Apache problem is. I knew that a righteous fool like Fenraw couldn't resist wreaking vengeance on the Chokonen after that trouble at the O'Brien place and now I know that removing those Indians will just take a little longer and require a bit more investment.'

'So Fenraw is surplus to requirements now,' said Ryker.

A sly smile danced across Cleets' face. 'I think Mr Canton is more than capable of carrying out the tasks we require in the future. A man of his temperament is perhaps more suited to the job.'

'And something of a local hero now that he's brought Fenraw and his rowdies to justice,' said Rogers. 'That can only help, surely.'

'It all falls into place Nate, all in good time,' the Mayor sat so far back in his chair that his feet lifted off the ground.

'You sly fox,' Ryker laughed quietly.

'With the will of the people behind us gentlemen there is nothing we can't achieve,' said Cleets smugly.

The three men puffed their cigars and sipped their whisky in silence for a few moments before Rogers stood up and walked to the coat stand for his jacket.

'Well gentlemen, I think we must all be in agreement that we have a lot to look forward to,' he said. 'Especially if Judge Stephenson is of the same mind.'

'He is with us,' said Cleets. 'And as soon as he gets back from wherever the hell he is, I will set him straight on the recent events.'

'He's got a queer taste for justice though,' said Ryker.

'Jed's right,' said Rogers with slight alarm. 'Maybe he'll give Fenraw's posse a generous hearing.'

Cleets leaned forward easily and reached for the whisky bottle.

'Gentlemen, gentlemen. You forget that in the absence of Mr Stephenson I have the power to administer both the law and any penalty for breaking it. And, if it makes you sleep a little easier, maybe we should commence the trial of Fenraw and his outlaws some time tomorrow. That way, Stephenson will have no say in their ultimately fatal punishment.'

'That sounds fine to me,' said Rogers. 'I'll bid you goodnight gentlemen.'

Cleets and Ryker raised their glasses to him.

'Good cheer Mr Rogers,' said Cleets. 'All in all I'd say it has been a very fine day.'

The first night-watchman at the stables behind the Blackwater Hotel was very fortunate. Silent's blade cut between his shoulder blades and ended his life in blissful ignorance. The second night-watchman felt a rush of fear when he saw his associate face down in the straw in a pool of blood, but darkness soon enveloped him as George Kelly emerged from behind a bale swinging the handle of an axe. George and Silent searched the bodies for weapons.

'Two pistols, a rifle and five horses,' hissed George. 'That's enough.'

Silent shook his head in disagreement, pointed outside the stable and moved out.

'God damn,' cursed George as he followed him.

The street was empty but the hum of conversation seeped from the Blackwater saloon. Silent and George clung to the shadows.

'So what's the plan?' said George.

Silent hushed him with a gesture and pointed at four men who had just left the bar. They were obviously some of Canton's latest recruits as most of them sported gun belts with two pistols and each one had a shotgun or rifle slung casually over his shoulder. They swaggered along the dusty main street, safe in the knowledge that now that Fenraw was behind bars they were part of Wilburg's law enforcement. Two days before they had been plain citizens but now they were a force to be reckoned with, or so they thought. Their bravado was increased further as they passed a bottle of whisky between themselves.

'Maybe we should pay a visit to Madame Bellende's,' muttered one of the men. 'Surely as peacekeepers we deserve a little sustenance.'

The oafs all laughed heartily and another spoke up. 'That's a fine idea. Just what we need before a little hanging tomorrow.'

The men had walked just beyond the main street and it was pitch dark. Madame Bellende's house of ill repute was kept a discreet distance from the centre of town but a warm, welcoming light from its windows was twinkling in the distance. Only a brief shaft of moonlight lit Silent's blade before it dug deep in the side of one of the men. Simultaneously, George Kelly's axe handle cracked the skull of another man and as both figures fell into the dust the remaining men stared frantically into the dark to see their attackers. Silent dropped to the ground and spun his leg in a sweeping movement right behind the knees of one of the survivors. The force of the blow lifted the man off his feet and he crashed down on his back. Before he could regain the breath that had been forced out of his body Silent's knife was deep in his chest. The last man standing had the build of a bear and George Kelly in his sights. He roared in anger and charged. Kelly swung his axe handle wildly but it only glanced the man's shoulder. There was a crunch of flesh and bone and George was on his back with beefy fists pounding his face. He fought back but the man was overpowering him. Silent leapt on the attacker's back and tried to take his blade to the man's throat but he was brushed off like a fly and thrown to the ground. George could feel his strength sapping and tried to jam his fingers into the stranger's eyes but the man just gripped his massive hands around George's throat and started to squeeze. Silent flayed his hands around in the dust, desperate to find his knife but it was lost in the darkness. He felt for George's axe handle but it to was nowhere to be found. He could hear his partner gasping frantically for breath so he did the only thing he could, he fired a single shot into the hulking figure's head. The man fell forward, crashing down onto George's chest. Kelly was too weak to move and only when Silent had pulled the brute off him could he begin to take short gasps of air into his aching lungs.

Silent stood in the darkness, his ears straining to hear if the solitary shot had drawn any attention. The town was quiet.

'You damn fool,' gasped George. 'We agreed. No shooting.'

Silent sneered and helped George to his feet.

'Give me... give me a minute,' wheezed George and then he realised how ungrateful he must have sounded. 'Thanks man, thanks.'

They stood together in the darkness, George regaining his breath and Silent peering back into town for any signs of life.

George recovered enough to plant a kick at his attacker's lifeless body.

'Ugly son of a bitch,' he wheezed.

Silent had already started to relieve the corpses of their weapons.

'That's it brother. We've got all we need now. Let's get back to the rest of them and get the hell out of town. If we didn't already have a date with the hangman we sure as hell do now.'

As the sun rose in Wilburg a small boy found four dead figures in the dust on the road to Madame Bellende's. Dried pools of blood were being blown away with the dust and buzzards had started to peck at the bodies. When the news reached town Canton, Dodge and a handful of their new recruits rushed to the jailhouse. Only Averill's tattered corpse remained, still strapped to a chair with his lifeless eyes staring at the wall.

The slaughter of the previous night soon had the whole population of Wilburg on the streets. Cleets wasted no time in spreading the word that all new recruits to the cause were to meet in the centre of town at the earliest opportunity. They gathered together like a ragtag army battalion and Canton immediately made the most of his opportunity

'What we have here is a complete breakdown of law and order in this good town,' said Canton as he strolled along his line of deputies. 'Douglas Fenraw and his mercenaries have chosen to side with those copper miners out of town to form a rebel group whose only goal is to harm the good people of Wilburg.'

There were a few half-hearted calls of approval and this was enough to drive Canton on to what he believed to be the most important address of his life.

'This threat to our liberty can only be met with one solution. We ride out today to bring down the weight of our town's law on all those who trespass against us. If we are successful, we will continue on to the Chokonen camp and demand that those savages find settlement elsewhere so that we can mine the rich deposits that are rightfully ours.'

There was a small ripple of puzzled conversation across the crowd. Canton felt a little dejected that his fine words had not garnered a better response.

'For God's sake Jim,' shouted Dodge in exasperation as he turned to face the mob. 'Get saddled up boys and let's kill Fenraw and those bastard McNairns. Then we move on to wipe those damned Apaches off the face of the earth and fill our pockets with gold.'

The mob roared, waved their guns in the air and ran to their steeds.

Canton looked at Dodge's leering face. 'Very effective Frederic. Crude but effective.'

Jumping on his horse, Canton realised that fancy words were wasted on these blood-thirsty thugs. Violence was all they understood and he had to make sure he lead from the front.

When Fenraw's gang reached the McNairn mine they were so exhausted that they failed to notice that their usual antagonistic welcome had all but disappeared. Billy McNairn and Nancy came to the door of the house and although Billy was sporting his usual frosty glare the appearance of Fenraw and partners did not raise any alarm. The miners continued with their work and Billy stepped down from the porch.

'Can't stay away from us now Fenraw,' said Billy with the smallest hint of a smile.

'It's not a visit I chose to make I'm afraid,' said Fenraw as he got off his horse. 'We've just busted out of Wilburg's jail and they've got us down as the killers from the O'Brien place. It's all bullshit but Cleets has got the dimwits from the town believing him and he's throwing money around to recruit every lowlife that can hold a gun.'

Billy's expression returned to its usual state, red and furious.

'So where the hell does that leave us?'

Fenraw said nothing and tried to catch Nancy's attention but she refused to meet his gaze.

'Tell him Douglas,' Fred shouted over.

'Tell me what?' yelled Billy.

'I think they believe that we have worked some deal together for the future. I'm not sure what they suspect but if it is anything like that then you are not safe here either.' Fenraw stared at the ground guiltily.

'Not safe? This is my damned land,' said Billy angrily. 'My family fought and died to get here. Where the hell can we go? '

'Maybe until this cools down…'

'Go to hell Fenraw. You are the one that brought this plague of greed to our door. Get back on your damn horse and keep moving.'

'That ain't going to make no difference Bill,' said Fred. 'If we go now that just leaves you short by five shooters. Cleets' mob may be ugly and green behind the ears but they are all armed and Canton has filled their minds with all sorts of crazy shit.'

'God damn you Fenraw,' said Billy. 'Things were bad when we first met you and they have been getting worse ever since. What the hell are we going to do? These are working men Fenraw. Some of them don't even have a gun.'

George Kelly was keeping his eyes on the horizon behind them. 'We have to do something Douglas. They ain't going to be far behind us.'

No one spoke for a while. Billy and Fenraw stared at each other but it was Nancy who broke the silence.

'For god's sake Bill bring them into the house.'

'Don't let your heart rule your head Nancy,' said Billy as he glared at Fenraw.

Nancy strutted down from the porch and pushed Billy on the shoulder.

'You two stags can't see what is happening through your hate for each other,' she said. 'My priority is helping to protect this mine that I've worked so damn hard for so leave your bullshit aside and let's talk about how the hell we are going to defend ourselves.' The two men stood their ground.

'Let's go,' Nancy shouted in exasperation and stormed back into the house. Billy followed her but shouted to one of the miners as he went. 'Get my brother over here now.'

'On you go boys,' George shouted over to Fenraw and Fred. 'Time is running out. Me, Jim and Silent will keep a lookout.'

Fenraw did not like taking orders from anyone. He stared into the wide plains that they had just travelled across. His head was swirling with different emotions. His hatred for Billy McNairn was growing again but to leave them, and leave Nancy, at the mercy of Canton's thugs was unthinkable. Even if they stayed then their chances of survival were slim and he had dragged them all to this point. Would the Kelly brothers and Silent be in a better position today if they had never even met him? The stench of death followed him wherever he went.

'Come on Douglas,' said Fred. 'You had better get a taste for diplomacy real quick or we are going to die out here in this damned hole in the dust.'

Fenraw only grunted as they made their way inside.

At the back of the large kitchen in the McNairn house Billy and Bobby were deep in conversation. As Fenraw and Fred entered the room McNairn ignored them and continued talking in an even quieter tone. When they had finished talking Bobby slipped out of the back door without even acknowledging the visitors.

'Where the hell is he going?' said Fenraw angrily.

'None of your damn business,' yelled Billy.

There was an almighty smash as Nancy threw the biggest bowl she could lay her hands on onto the floor.

'Stop. Just stop,' she screamed.

The room fell silent.

'All this damn arguing has not got us anywhere. Is it only going to stop when we are all dead?' Nancy's eyes were damp with tears but her face was red with anger. 'I promised that when Stuart died I would help make this place a new home for generations of McNairns to come but in the next hour it could be burnt to the ground and we could be just like the O'Briens... damn corpses. Yet all you two care about is tearing strips off each other.'

Nancy was shaking slightly and moving her glaring eyes between Billy and Fenraw who still said nothing. She darted towards the dresser and picked up her pistol and gunbelt.

'To hell with you both,' she cried. 'I'll meet them outside on my own.'

'Nancy no,' Fenraw tried to grab her but she slipped past him. Fred closed the door quickly and stood in front of it.

'Please Nancy,' he pleaded.

Nancy whipped her pistol from her holster swiftly and held it to Fred's head.

'Godammit, get out of my way or I'll put a bullet in you. You'll be dead soon enough anyway.'

Fenraw tried to grab Nancy and a pistol shot ran out. There was a splinter of wood and Fred dropped to his knees clutching the side of his head. Blood dripped through his fingers.

'My ear,' he yelled. 'Crazy bitch shot my ear.'

Nancy dropped the pistol in shock and by the time Jim and Silent burst through the door she was sobbing uncontrollably in Fenraw's arms.

Canton raised an arm in the air and drew his posse of thirty men to a halt at the foot of a small hill.

'Last stop Dodge,' he said to his partner. 'Get these men fed and watered because the next time they stop will be to put those damn miners in the ground for good.'

Dodge turned to face the ragtag occupants of wagons and horses who stared at him emptily, waiting for instructions.

'Drink your hooch, eat your chow and get them horses some water,' he yelled. 'Be ready to ride out in twenty minutes. It's time for some killing.'

Many of the men stared at Dodge blankly. They had not thought to bring any provisions and they barely had a pocket watch between them. Canton noticed their vacant stares and wondered if they had any idea what they were about to do. They were bumpkins with borrowed guns about to face Fenraw and his well-seasoned killers. He contented himself in the thought that these oafs could ride in front of him like a human shield. If any of them could shoot even half straight then himself, Dodge and the dozen or so experienced fighting men in the posse could finish the job. What were they up against anyway? A bunch of tunnel monkeys armed with spades and a damned woman?

Canton thought of his meeting with Nancy that day back in Wilburg. Along with Dodge and Averill they had cornered her in the provisions store and asked if she had any idea of Fenraw's whereabouts. She gave nothing away and when Dodge pinched her ass she gave him a slap the rattled the few teeth he had left in his head. He was set to kill her right there but Canton held him back. Maybe he would hold them all back once again and seek a little comfort from the widow McNairn once the heat of battle had died down.

'Jim. Jim,' Dodge's voice snapped Canton out of his seedy daydream.

'What?'

'You going to give these boys a little talk to pep them up?'

Canton was still a little unfocused. 'Eh? Oh yeh. Yeh, I've got something to say.'

Canton chose to stand on a large rock nearby to give his address a little gravity.

'Gentlemen, gentlemen, might I say a few words.'

No one was listening. Canton glared at Dodge.

'Everyone, shut your damn mouths and listen up to Mr Canton here,' Dodge roared.

With his audience suitably prepared, Canton began his speech. 'Gentlemen, I brought you all together because you are then finest group of men Wilburg has to offer and I believe that the money you have all been paid so far has been a wise investment.'

Like dupes in front of a snake-oil salesman they bought Canton's false praise and looked around at each other with proud smiles.

'What we are about to face are a rebel band of miners who are intent on withholding future riches that belong to Wilburg,' Canton continued. 'In fact, riches that you all deserve a share of as upstanding citizens of our fine town.' Canton was enjoying the attentive glare he was receiving from his posse and it spurred him on to elevate his simple speech to something closer to the Gettysburg address.

'Joining these immigrant thieves are the disgraced lawman Douglas Fenraw and his partners in crime. Partners that only last night butchered my dearest friend Clancy Averill and four other law-abiding citizens.'

There was a murmur of disapproval amongst the mob and some half-hearted shouts of encouragement.

'But what we do now friends is not revenge. No, we must face these bandits to protect everything we hold dear about our town. To protect our families from the greed that these miners perpetuate. To protect our future prosperity.'

Many of the posse were starting to tire of Canton's showboating and were getting a little restless. Two rallying speeches in one day was more than they were used to. Dodge signalled to Canton to bring the speech to a close.

'God is with us men,' said Canton. 'We are on the side of the law and I congratulate you all for making the right choice.'

A small ripple of hand-clapping drifted from the group. Dodge stepped forward and thrust his rifle into the air.

'Saddle up you dogs,' he yelled. 'Those damn miners are trying to take the food off our tables and the dollars from our pockets. Let's go and kill them all.'

The mob roared and made for their horses. The stirring emotions that Canton had felt disappeared into the wind but he felt a grudging admiration for his partners call to arms. Perhaps that was the only language these sons of bitches understood.

Silent stood guard at the window while Fenraw and the Kelly brothers sat at one side of the kitchen table facing Billy McNairn and a few of his men. Nancy stood beside them, too anxious and angry to sit down.

'Time is running out gentlemen,' she said angrily. 'You stubborn fools better throw your differences aside right now or we can all die right here.'

'Just give her a gun and send her out. Poor bastards won't stand a chance,' said Fred, nursing his bloody ear.

Fenraw glared at Billy over the table. 'How many guns do you have?'

'My men use tools not weapons Fenraw,' Billy barked back. 'We keep a half dozen rifles and a few shotguns around in case of trouble but god damn we ain't had no trouble until we met you. Now we got it in spades.'

'Why you ungrateful...' Fenraw growled.

Silent stopped Fenraw mid sentence by gesturing wildly for them to come to the window.

'Oh my god,' panted Nancy. 'Is this it?'

Jim Kelly was first to the window. 'Jesus Christ Fred, you got to see this.'

Fenraw and Fred stood up almost in unison with their pistols at the ready. They ran over to the other kitchen window and peered out. The miners had strapped an old wagon to two of the Kelly's horses and everyone that could fit on was disappearing towards the hills.

Fred Kelly smashed one of the window's panes.

'God damn deserters,' he yelled. 'Come back here and fight.'

Fenraw span round and glared at Billy once more.

'You let them go you bastard,' he hissed. 'That's where Bobby went... to tell them. You've signed our death warrant you old fool.'

'They are my men Fenraw. Miners not damn mercenaries. Why should they die just because of your mistakes.'

'You stupid old goat. I should kill you right now.' Fenraw moved towards Billy, his knuckles tightening around his pistol.

'Douglas, no!' screamed Nancy and threw herself at Fenraw. He caught her and they were locked in an embrace. 'Please, no more, please,' she sobbed. 'I can't take it.'

Fenraw's head was swimming. Nancy's frantic embrace unlocked emotions he had not felt for years but his hatred for Billy still burned inside him. There was a loud knock at the back door and everyone with a gun turned and took aim.

'Don't shoot, don't shoot,' yelled Billy. 'It's my men with the guns.'

'What men?' shouted Fred.

'Steven? Craig? Is that you?' said Billy as he moved towards the door.

'Let us in for Christ's sake, we can hear some horses out front.'

Billy pulled open the door and four men burst in. Each one carried heavy sacks which they threw on the kitchen table. The miner's arsenal slipped from the bags.

'Everyone grab a gun,' yelled Fenraw. 'And make sure it's loaded you damn hillbillies.'

Fred gestured to the new arrivals and looked at Billy. 'Is this it?'

'We're all here,' said Billy gravelly.

'Maybe this will help,' said Steven as he produced another bag and emptied its contents on the table. A pile of dynamite sticks rattled onto the heavy wooden surface. Each one had a short fuse, prepared for attack rather than rock blasting.

Silent waved Fenraw over to the window once again. Fenraw peered through the dirty glass at a small dust cloud in the distance.

'We've got company.' He cocked his rifle and the loud click silenced the room. 'Anybody got a battle plan?'

As the Wilburg posse approached the mine Canton turned round to look at his men and was discouraged to see that most of them were simply enjoying the view.

'Get your weapons ready,' he hissed. 'This ain't no damn day in the country.'

Dodge was obviously of the same mind as Canton and gestured to a small group of the men to ride forward. They were fools but not complete fools and they rode parallel to Canton and Dodge but no further. Some of the group began to look distinctly uneasy as they fully realised what they were actually about to partake in. They moved slowly forward but there was no resistance to be found. The closer they got the more clear it became that the camp was empty. There were no horses in sight and the door of the house flapped open in the gentle wind. All the huts and outbuildings looked empty. It was like the Marie Celeste. A small wisp of smoke slipped from the chimney of the Mc-Nairn house but nobody was in.

Canton visibly relaxed, then his chest started to swell a little. An easy victory to begin with. Fenraw and his friends had fled with the miners like rats from a sinking ship and he had secured the mine without one drop of blood. He gathered the men into a loose semi-circle in front of the house.

'Gentlemen, what we have here is a clear illustration of the power we wield as enforcers of the law. The men here would rather flee than face...'

His address was cut short by a fizzing stick of dynamite that sailed through the air in a wide arc and landed on the ground in front of the first four horses nearest the mine entrance. The hapless riders stared at the explosive for a second then moved their eyes towards Canton. The explosion forced them into the air and they fell to the ground as bloody corpses.

Every horse in the posse reared in fear and most of Canton's men were thrown to the ground.

'They are in the mine. Kill them,' screamed Dodge, pointing at the entrance to the mine.

The remainder of the posse fired wildly where Dodge had directed them. There was no one visible but they emptied their guns anyway.

'Hold on, hold on,' yelled Canton. 'Hold your fire, who the hell are you shooting at?'

The mob were reluctant to stop firing and before the shots died down completely the fizz of a dynamite stick was audible once again. This explosion sent another three men to their doom and the posse stared in horror at the mangled horses and dead bodies. Each man that could move retreated from the mine entrance even though the second stick had came from another direction.

'God damn you,' yelled Dodge as he spun his horse round looking for his attackers. 'Get out here and fight Fenraw.'

As the Wilburg men were plunged into a pit of confusion Bobby McNairn made the biggest mistake of his life. He was returning to the camp when he heard the explosions. He spurred his horse forward and as he galloped around a small hill next to the farm he came into plain view of the Canton's posse. Terrified and desperate to find the enemy, almost all of them took aim and fired. Most of them hit their target.

As Bobby's lifeless body hit the ground Billy McNairn's piercing wail could be heard from one of the huts near the mine entrance.

'There he is,' shouted Canton.

The posse focused their firepower on the hut and their bullets rattled through its wooden frame.

One of the miners leapt from behind another hut with a burning stick of dynamite in his hand. Dodge picked him off with his rifle before he could launch the explosive and the man fell back dropping the stick behind him. The sound of the charge exploding thundered around the mine once again and the hut disappeared in a ball of flame. Burning fragments landed on many of the other huts setting them alight immediately. Canton could hear panicking voices inside the huts and he grinned broadly.

The Wilburg men could sense that the tide was turning in their favour and blind fear changed to blood lust. Most of them trained their weapons on the huts where they could hear coughing and choking. They were ready for a turkey shoot.

'Take it easy boys,' said Dodge calmly as he motioned to his men to lower their guns. He was not ready for the slaughter to begin just yet.

'Throw your weapons out and show yourselves,' shouted Canton. 'You can face us like men or burn to death in those huts. Anyone else lurking behind a rock better break cover or we'll kill the first damn miners we see. That goes for you and your ingrates too Fenraw.'

The first to show himself was one of the remaining miners. He threw out his shotgun and stood up slowly from behind a rock that was remarkably close to the Wilburg posse. One of Canton's men put him down with a single bullet.

'God damn I said take it easy,' screamed Dodge and put a bullet of his own in the shooter's arm.

Canton glared furiously at the man who was clutching his bloody arm and rolling in the dust. Then he turned his attention back to the burning huts.

'Come on now Douglas, you ain't got much time.'

Fenraw was coughing furiously. 'What is this Canton? Execution? Maybe I'd be better to die in here you bastard.'

'No executions here Fenraw, I'm a reasonable man. Now throw out those guns and show yourselves.'

The huts were burning furiously now and Canton wondered if Fenraw and the miners would rather face the fire than him. Underneath the roar of the flames he could hear Fenraw shouting.

'Move out everyone,' wheezed Fenraw. 'Throw the guns out first and keep your hands high.'

Weapons were launched through the windows of two of the huts then the doors burst open. In the thick smoke that belched forth it was impossible to make out who was who but as the air cleared Canton could see Fenraw, Billy McNairn, the Kelly boys and Silent. All of them were on their knees in the dust gasping for breath. Behind them were two miners with a figure under a blanket. As the blanket dropped, Canton was filled with pleasure at the sight of Nancy McNairn. She was asphyxiated but otherwise unharmed and her full bosom was heaving wildly as she frantically filled her lungs with air.

Canton ordered his men off their horses and they formed a loose line in front of their opponents who were still wheezing on the ground.

Billy was struggling to breath but he crawled towards Canton gasping. 'You killed my brother you heathen...'

Dodge stepped forward and knocked Billy out with a single kick to the head.

'Take the woman into the house and don't harm her,' Canton said menacingly to two of his men. 'I'll be with her in a moment.'

Silent flew at Canton before Fenraw could but his pace was slower than usual and three of the posse grabbed him roughly and beat him to the ground.

'Damn you Canton you scum of the earth,' yelled Fenraw.

Canton levelled his pistol at Fenraw and dispassionately shot him in the knee. 'No damn you Fenraw you self-righteous fool.'

Fenraw dropped to the ground groaning in pain but refused to scream even though his whole body ached to cry out as he cradled his shattered knee cap and blood pulsed through the gaps in his fingers. Dodge laughed cruelly at Fenraw's agony and few others joined in.

'You could have had it all Douglas,' Canton continued. 'A share of this mine, a share of the gold... the woman. Now I've got it all and these good men here are going to share it with me.'

'You won't last a week,' croaked Billy. 'None of you know a damn thing about mining. You'll be buried alive.'

'There are tunnel monkeys dropping off the boats at California every day McNairn, only this time they will be working for me,' said Canton.

Canton noted with pleasure how close to the ground his opponents were trying to get. Fenraw, the Kelly's, Silent and the miners were almost flat in the dust now. He had broken them and they lay before them at his mercy. A few more words to rally his followers then he could shoot them where they lay and leave them there. Suddenly he noticed that Billy McNairn was actually grinning.

'What about the Chokonen Canton?' Billy said. 'Have you thought of them?'

'Damn Indians,' said Canton. 'If they are as easy to beat as you...'

His words faded into the wind as a bullet ripped through his neck and left him choking in his own blood. As Canton fell to his knees, Dodge and the rest of the posse spun round to see a line of Apaches the length of the horizon.

'Get back,' Fenraw hissed to his friends and they scuffled through the dust in search of cover.

For one second the Wilburg posse were startled like rabbits and frozen to the spot with fear at the sheer number of opponents before them. For many, the realisation of just what taking a dollar from Canton really meant came too late. Crazy to the end, Dodge pointed both his pistols at the Chokonen.

'Kill the savages,' he screamed.

Before he could fire his first shot a hail of bullets descended on them.

In the kitchen of the McNairn farmhouse the survivors slouched on the first chair or space on the floor that they could reach. Silent was standing near the window wiping blood from his mouth and Fenraw sat near the table with his wounded leg resting on another chair. Nancy was tending to his wound with some small tweezers.

'I ain't never pulled so many bullets from one man before,' she said as she removed the slug from Fenraw's knee.

'Sweet mother of...' hissed Fenraw at the sharp pain.

'Now, now Douglas,' laughed Fred Kelly. 'This is a respectable house. Let's not have that language in here.'

Despite Fenraw's obvious pain, Jim and George laughed too and even Silent's face broke into a smirk. Nancy dropped the bloodied, bullet onto the table.

'Sorry, but this one ain't gold.'

Fenraw groaned in agony and reached for a whisky bottle. Nancy pushed the bottle over to within his reach and dipped a clean bandage in some iodine.

'You better take a deep draught of that honey, this is going to sting a little,' she said before applying the dressing gently.

'Jesus Christ,' cursed Fenraw as the sharp pain added to the agony he already felt.

Fred laughed again. 'He can't help you brother but you got a good woman there to soothe you.'

Nancy blushed a little and patted Fenraw's arm comfortingly. 'I've done all I can but you really need a doctor.'

'We'll ride back to town and get help,' said George.

Jim looked startled. 'What about the Apaches.'

'Hell, McNairn's still out there with them now,' replied George. 'They ain't killed him yet. What the hell is going on?'

'What has that old goat done?' Fenraw said to Nancy. 'Are you McNairns a new Apache tribe?'

'There are other ways of dealing with people than shooting them Douglas,' she sighed.

'Hey maybe we should try that Fenraw,' joked Fred. 'Sure as hell haven't got far just by killing folks.'

Fenraw's men were in high spirits but it was simply an adrenalin rush from still being alive. They had been attacked, near burnt to death then witnessed the slaughter of Canton's posse first hand. Not a man from Wilburg was left alive but they were untouched. The Chokonen never intended to kill a single one of the McNairns and as they had been in the dust beside them their lives had also been spared.

Fenraw winced in pain and reached for the whisky.

'I'll go and get the doc,' said George rising from his chair.

Silent signalled to George to stay in his chair and gestured that he would go alone.

'Are you sure?' said Fenraw. He saw that Silent's eyes were deadly serious. He had noticed that look before and it usually meant that someone was about to get hurt.

'Come here,' said Fenraw.

When Silent was close enough Fenraw grabbed his partner's shirt and pulled him closer.

'You make sure you get back here. And in one piece.'

Silent smiled and as he broke from Fenraw's grip they shook hands. Silent nodded to Nancy and the Kellys then went out the back door.

'Do you think a doctor will come back with him?' said Jim.

'They won't have no choice,' Fenraw smiled. 'Mr Silent don't take no for an answer.'

'You sure pick up some unusual strays Fenraw,' said Fred.

'Why do you think I ended up working with you?' replied Fenraw.

'I don't know, but a crazy mute that looks like a bum but fights like a General? That is one odd fella,' said Fred as he reached for the whisky.

'Have you been friends for a while,' asked Nancy.

Fenraw stared into the distance a little. 'I think I knew him way back but I can't remember when. If it was him, it was certainly before his accident. His damn tongue may be missing but I'm sure he could say a little something if he chose to. Probably spent so much time on his own that he has forgotten how to.'

Billy and the two remaining miners entered the kitchen. Through the open door Fenraw could see the Chokonen tribe disappearing in the distance.

'Well, well Mr McNairn,' said Fenraw. 'Still got your scalp?'

'Those people ain't savages Fenraw. Just people with families just like us,' replied Billy as he took a seat at the table.

The mention of families brought a heaving guilty feeling down on Fenraw's chest once again. He dropped his head in shame. 'I know McNairn, I'm sorry.' The words almost burned his throat but he was glad that they had slipped out, however grudgingly.

Nancy noticed Fenraw's change of mood and squeezed his hand. Even that gentle touch lifted Fenraw's spirits a little.

'They are more reasonable than those rats from Wilburg and they saved our damn lives,' said Billy.

'Is that where Bobby went? To get the Apaches?' asked Fred.

At the mention of his brother's name Billy's shoulders drooped and he scowled hard to keep his eyes dry.

'Bobby and I went to see them after you attacked them. I wanted them to know that we had nothing to do with that,' said Billy.

'That was either very brave or very stupid,' said Fenraw.

'Well it worked a damn sight better than rolling down that hill and shooting their womenfolk.' Billy seemed to welcome the distraction of arguing with Fenraw again. 'I thought they were going to have my head on a stick at first but their leader, Teboca, seemed kind of impressed that we had come alone and unarmed.'

'You walked into the Chokonen camp without a gun?' said Fred incredulously. 'After what we did?'

'I had to do something dammit. I knew that if I didn't act they would ride out seeking vengeance and we were the first white folks in their way. I promised Teboca that I would lead the O'Brien's killers here then let him know. Make sure that the people who started this damn trouble got what was coming.'

Fenraw's fury temporarily blanked out the pain in his leg and he got to his feet.

'You mean you used us as damned bait to draw Canton's men here?' he shouted.

'I knew you would be back here anyway to hang round my sister-in-law like a bad smell.'

The pain was too great for Fenraw to think of a suitable comeback and he dropped back into the chair with a deep groan.

'Draw the wasp to the sweet honey. I like it,' said Jim with a smile.

'Go to hell,' retorted Fenraw then he saw that Nancy was blushing.

'You are lucky that Chokenen chief was so reasonable,' yelled Billy. 'He could just as easily have killed us all.'

'Then why didn't he?' asked George.

'Because I offered to help them mine their gold,' said Billy quietly.

'You what?' said Fenraw.

'I offered to help them. Our skills, their seam. We agreed a share of the profits.'

'You old fool,' sneered Fenraw. 'They will let you dig the gold out then bury you all in the rubble.'

'I don't think so,' said Billy as he walked over to a battered wooden chest that sat next to the fireplace. It looked like a storage box for firewood but when Billy lifted the lid it was filled with dirty gold nuggets, some as big as a fist.

'Sweet Jesus,' gasped Jim.

'You've had that here all the time,' asked Fred in amazement.

'That's just a sample,' said Billy. 'Just a few of the bits they could pull out of the ground with some simple tools.'

'So what is this? A pay-off?' said Fenraw grimly.

'God damn Fenraw,' spat Billy furiously. 'This is just a gesture of goodwill, something you know damn all about. We are going to help them mine that seam and share the profits fairly.'

'What are a bunch of Apaches going to do with the money,' said Fenraw. 'You can only buy so many beads and blankets.'

Billy sat down again shaking his head.

'You've got a low opinion of everyone Fenraw. I pity you. Money is the only thing that counts for anything out here. They know which way the wind is blowing. They are going to use it to buy their land, and secure it for future generations. And they need medicines, supplies, cabins... maybe it's God's way of rewarding them for living so hard yet giving their land so much respect.'

'And what about the gold bullets?'

'Hell, they won't be using them no more,' Billy laughed. 'Once they have money I'm sure they will invest in some more weapons. They ain't stupid. They ain't going to let parasites like Cleets try to take from them again.'

'It will work Douglas,' said Nancy resting her hand gently on Fenraw's shoulder. 'The Chokonen are good people. We can make a good living with them, more than enough to free us from the clutches of Wilburg. That's just a town of widows and old men now anyway. They've got nothing.'

'You ain't wrong there Nancy,' said Fred.

'Stay with us, all of you,' she continued.

'And do what?' said Fenraw sharply.

'There will be plenty of work Fenraw and we will need to keep both mines secure,' said Billy. 'Hell you might even find something you are good at other than killing.'

Fenraw sat quietly and everyone else in the room seemed to be waiting for an answer. He reached over his shoulder and gave Nancy's hand a little squeeze.

'I'll think about it.'

Doctor Max Harris lay on the rough wooden boards of a creaking wagon, shivering through a combination of the cold night air and sheer fear. He had been dragged from his home at knifepoint and been bound and gagged. He vaguely recognised his fair-haired aggressor from around town but the man had not spoken a word or offered any explanation for his abduction. Instead he had been bundled in to the wagon and driven around town. The kidnapper had made three stops already and each journey ended with another blood-soaked body being dumped in the wagon alongside him. Nate Rogers, Jed Ryker and Judge Stephenson lay close to his feet. All were stone, cold dead but their bodies were still warm and bleeding. The wagon came to a halt once more and through a small crack in the wooden side of the wagon he could see the council chambers.

'Hellfire,' yelled Mayor Cleets as he was woken from his slumber by a loud knocking on the door. 'What kind of damn fool comes visiting at this unearthly hour?'

The banging on the council chamber's door continued. Cleets was halfway down the candlelit staircase before he truly came to his senses and returned to the bedroom for his pistol. It was empty and as he struggled to load six bullets into the gun with his cold, bony hands, the banging on the door only frustrated him further.

'Jesus Christ,' he muttered. 'It must be that jack ass Canton. I could have killed those damn Indians quicker myself.'

The banging stopped but the mayor continued down the stairs anyway.

'Canton? Is that you?'

There was a single muffled shout of some sort outside. As the mayor un-locked the door he prepared to give his itinerant employee a double-barrelled dressing down. All he saw was Silent's inexpressive face, a glint of moonlight reflecting on his blade then darkness.

It was late in the evening and Fenraw was in Nancy's room propped up on her bed with two large duck down pillows behind him. A small log burner was glowing in the corner of the room. Whenever he had a moment to reflect his mind always drifted back to that dreadful night when he lost Jessie and Jimmy back in Breckenridge. Riding his horse to the point of exhaustion, sleeping in the dust and keeping the law with extreme prejudice were all things that, however unpleasant, kept the dark thoughts from the returning. Sure he enjoyed a joke with the Kelly brothers and being with Silent gave him a certain sense of familiarity but whenever things got quiet the torment began again.

This time though he had Nancy close by him and being here with her had the power to push away the despair. This was something new. Something he had not shared since he was with Jessie, and then the mere thought of his wife brought the dark thoughts flooding back. It was exhausting. Nancy tapped gently on the door then walked in with a hot cup of coffee and a bowl of soup.

'Has the doctor gone?' asked Fenraw.

'Yes he has,' she smiled. 'Poor bastard. We gave him a horse to get back to town but he seemed so scared I reckon he would have ran back if we had let him.'

'Silent can have that effect on people,' said Fenraw as he looked down at the fresh bandage on his knee. Nancy was hovering beside the bed.

'Why did you knock the door there? It's your home,' said Fenraw.

'I didn't know what you were up to,' replied Nancy coyly.

Fenraw smirked a little. 'What the hell would I be up to with a busted leg and a body full of bullet holes?'

Nancy put the cup and bowl down on a nearby table and sat on the edge of the bed.

'What would you like to be up to?' she said softly.

Fenraw could see that all traces of dust and smoke had been washed away and her black hair was glossy and smooth once again. Her skin glowed and a sweet fragrance surrounded her. Fenraw could feel his senses being inflamed and she was so close to him that he could feel the warmth of her body. Her full red lips were inches away from his and although it sent shards of pain through his body he lifted himself towards her. Their lips met and they were soon locked in a warm embrace. Nancy leaned over Fenraw with an urgent desire and he slid his hands beneath her rough workshirt, onto her smooth stomach and up towards her firm bosom. Nancy stood up sharply and pulled off every stitch of clothing. Her naked form was warmly lit by the glow of the small bedside lamp as she pulled back the bedsheet sharply and lowered herself onto Fenraw tantaslingly slowly. He gasped as if some long-forgotten sensations were suddenly flooding back into his brain and he felt every muscle stiffen. As their bodies locked together on the soft sheets the stinging pain in Fenraw's body was replaced with hot wave of passion.

Later that evening Fenraw again woke up screaming and in a cold sweat.

The piercing scream of Mayor Cleets' secretary travelled far across Wilburg through the early morning silence. Soon a small crowd had gathered outside the council chambers. Only gentle weeping and hushed, confused conversations could be heard. Propped up against the building's ornate doors were four of the town's most respected elders. Their throats had been cut and their cotton nightshirts were drenched in blood.

Nancy wandered downstairs, wrapped in a silk shawl and smiling contentedly. Billy McNairn was sitting at the kitchen table nursing a mug of coffee.

'Hell woman, what time of the morning do you call this,' he said with a smile.

'Good morning to you too brother-in-law,' she said as she dropped into an easy chair near the stove.

'What the hell was that fool Fenraw doing shouting in the night?'

'Just bad dreams Billy, he is plagued with them. Maybe he just needs a little rest.'

'And a little loving, eh?' said Billy wryly.

'Maybe some of that too brother-in-law,' sighed Nancy.

One of the miners burst into the kitchen and shattered Billy and Nancy's gentle conversation.

'Fenraw's leaving,' he blurted out. 'He's riding off with the mute.'

Fenraw and Silent were still strapping their rifles to their horses when Nancy burst from the house with Billy close behind.

'Douglas, wait,' she yelled.

The shout alerted the Kellys who peered from the window of their hut then strode over to investigate.

'Where the hell you going Douglas?' shouted Fred.

'I got to go fellas,' said Fenraw as he continued to tighten the saddle on his horse. 'That shit back in Breckinridge won't let me be.'

'You didn't find out anything before you left there,' yelled Fred. 'What the hell is different now?'

'Nothing, but I've got to try and find out more.'

'See? I told you,' said Jim Kelly, turning to his brother. 'He don't give a damn about us. Man, now the job is done he was not even going to say goodbye.'

'That's not how it is,' said Fenraw but Jim was already walking away in disgust.

'Godammit Fenraw, ain't you even going to stay till we bury my brother?' asked Billy in disbelief.

Nancy was sobbing openly. Any pretence that her feelings for Fenraw were indifferent had disappeared.

'My mind won't let me be,' said Fenraw as he continued packing his horse. He could not bring himself to make eye contact with any of them. 'Until I know who killed my family I'm no good to no one,' said Fenraw. 'I'm burning inside and I got to put that to rest first.'

'That's revenge Douglas,' pleaded Nancy. 'That is all that is and it will eat you up inside. You can wander the country forever and never find what you are looking for. Stay with us. Start again.'

'I just got to do this Nancy. I'll be back.'

Behind her tears Nancy was steadily growing more angry. 'No you won't. You'll chase these ghosts until you are too wounded to carry on. If you leave now you won't ever be back.'

Fenraw paused for a moment. Every nerve in his body screamed for Nancy's warm touch. He wanted to embrace her again, hold her tight and tell her he would stay but the vengeance he felt was too strong. Until he could bring his brand of justice to Jessie and Jimmy's killers he knew he could never be at peace.

'I'm sorry Nancy,' was all he could bring himself to say.

'Go to hell you son of a bitch,' she screamed and ran towards the house sobbing.

'I thought that deep inside of you there was at least a shred of decency Fenraw, but I was wrong,' growled Billy McNairn as he started to follow her. 'If I ever see you again it will be through the sight of a rifle.'

Silent got on his horse and Fenraw, Fred and George stared at the dust.

Fred broke the awkward silence. 'You done messed up this time Douglas. What the hell are you thinking about? You've got a beautiful woman here, a good job and some money at last. Why do you have to go on killing?'

'I've got to do this,' said Fenraw quietly. 'For my family.'

'Your family is gone Fenraw. You have to start living for yourself,' said George then quickly regretted what he had said as he saw Fenraw's eyes glow with fury.

'I'll never forget them,' hissed Fenraw.

'You don't have to forget them brother,' reasoned Fred. 'But you can't let what happened to them eat away at your soul.'

Fenraw said nothing and stared into the distance.

'Jesus Christ you are a stubborn old fool,' said Fred eventually as he thrust his hand forward. 'You stay safe Douglas. We will wait back here for you and make sure we keep your share of the gold.'

Fenraw shook Fred's outstretched palm then got on his horse.

'You take care of him friend,' Fred shouted to Silent.

'Yeh, that old bullet magnet is liable to get you both killed,' joked George.

Silent smiled and waved goodbye but there was real sadness in his eyes.

'Tell Nancy I...' Fenraw struggled to find the right words.

'I know brother, I know,' said Fred.

Fenraw and Silent rode away quickly and never looked back. Fred and George stood still and let the dust cloud kicked up by the horses drift over them.

'Do you think that is the last we'll see of them?' said George.

'I don't know,' answered Fred. 'But Fenraw is a hard man to kill.'

Fenraw and Silent had been riding for days despite the burning heat. They forced their horses on giving them water but little rest. Fenraw had barely slept or eaten at all. He demanded that they push on to their destination and Silent meekly followed, even though he was on the point of exhaustion. In his weary state he failed to notice how often Fenraw was glaring at him throughout their journey.

The heat was taking its toll on Fenraw's mind as well. All he could think about was the night his wife and son were killed. Vile images flashed through his head and he screwed his eyes up tight, trying to mentally focus on the faces of their tormentors. There were flashes of features but were these memories or just random faces? His family's killers or just some of the many pieces of human flotsam that he had sent to meet their maker in the name of the law? He could picture Jessie on the floor, her face streaked with blood and spitting something fleshy onto the floor as her fair-haired attacker screamed in pain. For years he had willed himself to focus. What was it? A finger? An ear? A tongue? He knew now.

Silent pulled his horse up sharply. As Fenraw stopped beside him he pointed at a small gathering of huts in the distance. Fenraw had at least expected a small town but this was no more than a glorified work camp.

'Is that it?' said Fenraw. Silent nodded and stared at Fenraw with a look of resignation in his eyes.

Fenraw felt a wave of relief overcome him but a rush of anger was not far behind. The vengeance he was searching for was almost in his reach.

'Give me the note,' he shouted to Silence.

Silent reached into his shirt pocket and passed over a crumpled piece of paper. Fenraw unfolded it roughly and glared at the two names on it.

'All these weeks together and you knew,' croaked Fenraw. 'All the times you had the opportunity to see me dead... it doesn't all make sense friend.'

Silent tried to force out some words and the dry, gargling sound shocked Fenraw with its unfamiliarity.

What?' said Fenraw.

Silent gestured to him to turn the paper over. Fenraw noticed a faint message written on the other side in what looked like a childish scrawl: "We all do bad things and we all have to pay in the end".

Fenraw could barely lift his eyes off the page as a great sadness enveloped him.

'Yes we do friend,' he said quietly. 'Yes we do.'

Fenraw drew quickly and fired a single bullet into his partner's chest. As Silent's lifeless body hit the ground Fenraw was already charging towards the settlement.

END